Abby was engrossed  seem to notice Luke's reaction. When on earth had Abby had a child? And why didn't he know about it?

For a second, just for the tiniest second, a wild thought flitted through his brain. He tried to approximate Reuben's age. Was he around four? Could, by some miracle, Reuben be his?

Almost as soon as the thought appeared, he shook it off. He was infertile. Tests had shown beyond any doubt that he was infertile. Reuben could never be his child. So whose child was he? And just how quickly had Abby moved on?

He cleared his throat, attracting her attention. 'You have a son.'

'Yes, yes I do.' Abby turned Reuben around in her lap to face Luke with a proud smile on her face. 'Reuben, this is Mommy's friend. He's called Luke and he's a doctor—like Mommy.'

Luke watched the little figure Abby had clutched closely to her chest. His heart was beating frantically. "Pleased to meet you, Reuben." He held his hand out to the little guy.

"How old is Reuben, Abby?

"He's four," she answered quickly.

Four. A new sensation flitted through him. She'd replaced him almost instantly.

Fury started to build inside him. All rational thought was leaving the building. He was infertile. He couldn't have kids. That was the reason he'd broken up with her—because he couldn't fulfil her dreams of having a family. And he hadn't wanted to make her lose that chance.

And she obviously hadn't. Abby had moved on and had the family she deserved. So why did it hurt so much?

Dear Reader

Do you remember 'the one that got away'? Everyone apparently has one and that's what this story is all about. Luke Storm and Abby Tyler have both taken different paths in life, but a set of extraordinary circumstances brings them together again and makes them realise what they've lost. However five years is a long time and the circumstances of both have changed, can they really rekindle what they had? As in any good medical romance the path of true love doesn't run smoothly!

This is my second book for Mills & Boon Medical™ Romance and I'm still very new and excited about being part of this line. One thing I've always loved about the medical romance line is the wide range of professions and settings that can be used. There is always the challenge of trying to find something that hasn't been used before and I relished the opportunity of setting this story around the White House Medical Service and their staff.

Please let me know what you think at www.scarlet-wilson.com

Many thanks

Scarlet

THE BOY WHO MADE THEM LOVE AGAIN

BY
SCARLET WILSON

First published in Great Britain 2011
by Mills & Boon, an imprint of Harlequin (UK) Limited.
Large Print edition 2012
Harlequin (UK) Limited, Eton House,
18-24 Paradise Road, Richmond, Surrey TW9 1SR

ISBN: 978 0 263 22457 3

Harlequin (UK) policy is to use papers that are
natural, renewable and recyclable products and made
from wood grown in sustainable forests. The logging
and manufacturing process conform to the legal
environmental regulations of the country of origin.

Printed and bound in Great Britain
by CPI Antony Rowe, Chippenham, Wiltshire

Scarlet Wilson wrote her first story aged eight and has never stopped. Her family have fond memories of 'Shirley and the Magic Purse' with its army of mice, all with names beginning with the letter 'm'. An avid reader, Scarlet started with every Enid Blyton book, moved on to the *Chalet School* series and many years later found Mills and Boon.

She trained and worked as a nurse and health visitor, and currently works in public health. For her, finding Medical™ Romance was a match made in heaven. She is delighted to find herself among the authors she has read for many years.

Scarlet lives on the West Coast of Scotland, with her fiancé and their two sons.

Check out Scarlet's fantastic debut

IT STARTED WITH A PREGNANCY

Also available in ebook format from www.millsandboon.co.uk

This book is dedicated to my mum and dad,
Joanne Barrie Wilson and John Niven Wilson,
who are, in fact, the best mum and dad in
the world. They've raised three daughters
who love them very much and cared for
and nurtured six grandchildren with
endless patience. Whenever either of my sons
come out with a 'fascinating fact'
I know where it came from!

CHAPTER ONE

IF ABBY TYLER had known how the day was going to end she might not have got out of bed that day.

As it was, she leaned back in her chair, arched her back and then did something that she never did—put her feet up on the desk. Pelican Cove was quieter than quiet. She hadn't treated a patient in the last hour.

She took a sip of the strong, dark coffee she'd just made and nibbled on one of the nearby home-made oatmeal and raisin cookies. She gave a huge sigh and smiled over at one of the nearby nurses. 'Nancy, you make the best cookies.' Abby closed her eyes for a second. Recovery time. Reuben had woken at three a.m. and came through to tell her a story. The story had lasted the best part of an hour and had been full of animal noises and hand gestures. It seemed as though she'd been blessed with a child who didn't require much sleep. Through her heavy lids she could see the rest of the emergency-room staff giving her knowing nods and moving off to the far end of the reception desk. The staff here were a great, tight-knit team with a real community approach.

As an emergency-care paediatric physician Abby loved the twelve weeks a year that she covered in the community hospital—in fact, it was one of the reasons that she'd taken the job. San Francisco was much more frantic. This gave her the opportunity to do some much-needed paediatric outpatient clinics and practise emergency medicine.

There was a screech of tyres outside. It startled her, breaking her from the easing, gentle lullaby that had been repeating in her head. Seconds later a pair of heavy feet pounded inside. The dark business suit, crisp white shirt, flash red tie and shock of white-blond hair drew the immediate attention of the surrounding staff.

Abby blinked. Twice. Before breaking into a lazy smile and brushing the cookie crumbs from her scrubs. 'Luke Storm. I always knew some day you'd come walking back through my door. I never doubted that. Something made it inevitable.' The words were out of her mouth in an instant. An automatic natural reaction to him, adapted from a film they'd watched together as med students. She ran her eyes up and down his muscular frame. Still every bit the male model. 'So what can I do for you?'

'You can take your feet off the desk for a start.'

'Excuse me?'

'I take it you work here?'

Abby gestured to the white board on the wall with her name on it. 'I take it I do,' she answered calmly, refusing to let him rile her.

'What facilities do you have for premies?'

That got her attention. 'What?' She pulled her feet off the desk and stood up. 'What on earth are you talking about?'

'I don't have time for a debate, Abby. I need to know if you can deal with a premature delivery or not. And I need to know *now*.'

Abby watched in disbelief as her calm emergency unit was instantly transformed into a scene of chaos. Half a dozen dark-suited men, some with obvious bulges in their jackets, swarmed through the doors and immediately started covering exits whilst muttering into small silver dots on their lapels and holding their earpieces. 'What on earth…?'

Luke grabbed hold of her arm. 'What facilities do you have, Abby?'

Abby shrugged her arm from his firm grasp. Her brain shifting sharply into focus. 'This is a small 25-bed acute-care hospital, Luke. It's mainly used for routine surgeries and outpatient consultations. We have this emergency department and we have equipment for emergency deliveries but we only have one neonate cot. Once stabilised we tend to transfer to San Francisco Children's Hospital.'

'Do you have a paed?'

It was obvious Luke wasn't thinking straight. What on earth had rattled him so much? Abby tilted her head, a smile dancing across her lips. His words were rapid and harsh and she could see from the deep frown lines in his forehead that a million different things were spinning around in his head. An expression she'd seen more than once.

Her pale-skinned hand reached across the desk and squeezed his golden tanned one. Like chalk and cheese. The way they'd always been with each other. '*I'm* the paed, Luke.'

His head turned abruptly towards her. 'You're the paed?' She could almost see the pieces falling into place in his head as the moment of realisation struck him. 'Of course you are. Then it's you that I need.' His hand closed around hers, pulling her towards the door. Just for a second she saw the characteristic gleam in his eyes that she remembered so well. 'Don't suppose you've got an obstetrician handy?'

'Actually, I do.' She ground to a halt, stopping him in his tracks. 'But I've no intention of phoning him until you tell me exactly what's going on. I take it you've got a patient for me?'

'Actually, I've got two—but the second one I can take care of myself.'

'What do you mean?' This was getting more bizarre by the minute.

'He's a cardiac patient. Where do you transfer your MIs to?'

She tugged on his hand. 'Stop, Luke,' she said in a low voice, and pulled him closer to her. Her senses were bombarded by the smell of him, bringing back fragments of past memories. But something was different. A new scent. A new cologne. Something fresh and sharp, reminding her of the crashing waves in the sea. She inched even closer. She could see the deep-etched frown lines on his brow, the tiny beads of perspiration glistening under the hospital lights. 'Slow down and take a deep breath and tell me what's going on.'

She heard him let out a deep sigh before he glanced over at one of the dark-suited men, who gave him a tiny nod of approval. He ran his fingers through his short white-blond hair, his eyes glancing at the ceiling, with one corner of his lip curling upwards. 'You're about to deliver the First Lady's baby.'

'What?'

Luke watched the colour rise in the unflappable Abby Tyler's cheeks. Her head flicked from side to side. 'I'm being had, right? This is one of those daft game shows, isn't it? You've got a hidden camera somewhere, haven't you?'

Luke stood stock still. He still quite couldn't believe that fate had brought him to an emergency unit that was staffed by Abby Tyler. Of all the places in all the world…

Abby put her hands on her hips. 'Luke, what on earth would the First Lady be doing in Mendocino Valley? Isn't she supposed to be on bed rest in the White House?'

Luke nodded and smiled wryly. 'That's what the

world is supposed to think. The truth is Jennifer Taylor would never have stayed on bed rest in the White House, which is why she's here.'

Abby shook her head. She couldn't believe this was happening. And she hadn't worked out what was more incredible to her—the fact the First Lady was in Mendocino Valley and nobody knew, or the fact that Luke Storm had just catapulted his way back into her life. She pulled her professional head back on. 'How far along is she? Thirty? Thirty-two weeks?' Abby's mind whirred, trying to remember what she'd seen in the press.

'She's just under thirty-two weeks.'

'Where on earth has she been staying and how come no one knows about it?'

Luke smiled. 'She's been staying in one of the mansions in the hills around here—I think you call it "Millionaires' Row"?' He named a hugely popular rock star who owned one of the nearby houses. 'Apparently he's good friends with the President and offered his house to them. His staff are very loyal and word just hasn't gotten out.'

'But how did she get here?' He could see her mentally calculating the distance in her head between Mendocino Valley and Washington before coming to the obvious conclusion. 'Who on earth let a woman in her condition fly?'

Luke gave a snort. 'You haven't met Jennifer Taylor yet, have you? Prepare yourself. And remember, she didn't exactly fly commercial. And she had her own obstetrician with her.'

Abby's face clouded in puzzlement. 'Well, where the hell is he?'

'He's the MI I'm about to treat.' Abby shook her head at the unfolding scene around her.

And he watched her. Drinking up her appearance, just for a second. The long sheen of blonde hair that he remembered had been cut into a sharp bob, short at the back with tapering longer layers at the front. It suited her, highlighting her high cheekbones and clear skin. He caught a waft of something. Strawberries. His eyes fell to her glistening pink lips. She was still using the same strawberry lip gloss that she'd used all those years ago. It gave him an instant reminder of kissing her and tasting that sweet, juicy gel, sending waves of nostalgia down his spine. His eyes swept over her body. Even hidden in shapeless green scrubs he could see the outline of her small breasts and neat hips. Perfection couldn't be hidden. And in amongst all his panic and confusion a wave swept over him—something that only Abby had ever done to him. He felt as if he had just come home.

His eyes fell to their hands, still tightly clasped. When was the last time he had held Abby's hand? Had it been the night she'd broken up with him? When she'd said she wouldn't give up on her dream of a family? Had that really been five years ago?

'Luke?'

Her voice pulled him back from memory lane. His head flicked around and he pulled her towards the doors and grabbed a nearby gurney. 'Come with me, Abby.'

She stopped, just for a second, and glanced towards the open-mouthed staff. 'Nancy, set up for an early delivery, please.'

She grabbed hold of the rail on the gurney and followed as he pulled it outside towards a sleek black car. The fresh sea winds immediately caught her hair, tossing and turning it before landing it back on top of her head like freshly whipped meringue. She tried to push the tangled mess from her eyes as she took in the scene in front of her.

Six black-suited men were strategically positioned around the car, their eyes scanning in every possible direction. The faint whoop-whoop of helicopter blades could be heard in the distance. A craggy-faced man put his hand on Luke's arm as his eyes ran up and down the full length of her body, 'Who's this?' The voice was brusque and gruff.

'Our saviour.' Luke's eyes caught hold of Abby's and she took a deep breath. Five years on and nothing had changed. He could still stop her heart with one look. And it killed her. Because everything *had* changed.

The nearside door was open and Luke gestured for her to look inside. She bent forward, removing more blonde strands of hair from her mouth, and peered inside.

'You're not going to put me on that, are you?' The words were straight to the point with only the slightest hint of strain in them.

Abby smiled at the pale face ahead of her and ducked inside the car out of the sea winds. 'Hi, I'm Abby, one of the doctors at Pelican Cove.' The spacious interior of the car nearly made her laugh out loud. Her entire Mini Cooper could fit inside the rear passenger space. She slid along the cream

leather seats and looked at the familiar face next
to her.

Jennifer Taylor was the darling of the nation. A
feisty, intelligent lawyer, she had refused to stop
working when her husband had become President.
She campaigned tirelessly for human rights and
wasn't afraid to put her neck on the line when
necessary. More importantly, she was also the first
First Lady in nearly fifty years to deliver while
her husband was in office.

Abby took in her short gasps, her grey jogging
suit and trainers and her normally immaculate
brown hair pulled back into a ponytail. The press
would have a field day if they saw her like this—
in all the news reports Abby had never seen this
woman with so much as a hair out of place. She
could see the worry lines across her brow and
the fatigue in her eyes. She leaned over and took
her hand. 'I think the gurney is for the other guy.'
She nodded in the direction of the sweating, grey-
haired man whom Luke was trying to assist out
of the front passenger seat. 'Do you want me to
get you a wheelchair or do you think you can
walk in?'

Jennifer looked up through her heavy eyes with steely reserve. 'I'm walking.'

'Okay, let me help you.' Abby slid back along the leather upholstery and waited for Jennifer to swing her legs from the car. She slid an arm around her waist and guided her inside, surrounded on all sides by the black brigade.

Nancy met her at the entrance door and gestured towards a nearby side room. 'I've set up in here,' she said, pointing her to the room, which had been hurriedly filled with monitoring equipment.

Luke gave a shout at her back as the gurney went speeding past and into the nearby trauma room. Abby watched thankfully as one of her nurse practitioners gave her a quick nod and followed Luke into the room.

Abby settled Jennifer on the bed and swung her legs up. She pulled out the backrest and watched in amusement as Nancy refused entry to any of the bodyguards. 'Wait outside, gentlemen. You can't be in here while the lady is being examined.' She shut the door with a quick slam and turned to face them, folding her arms across her chest. 'They won't get past me.'

Abby switched on the monitors and started

hooking them up. 'So tell me, Mrs Taylor, what's been happening today?' She turned her head to Nancy. 'Can you take a BP reading and get me a foetal heart rate, please?'

Jennifer shifted uncomfortably on the bed. 'Call me Jennifer, please, I hate formality. I started having back pain last night. Nothing major, just a general feeling of unease and nothing I could do would make me feel any better. Then at around breakfast time today, just after I'd used the bathroom, I felt a little trickle run down my leg.'

'Your waters have broken?'

'I think so. Dr Blair was going to check for me but then he started getting chest pain and...' Her voice tailed off as tears brimmed in her eyes. 'This isn't supposed to happen. I'm only meant to be here to rest for a few weeks and then I was going to go back to Washington to have the baby there.' She lay back against the pillows, resting her hands on her swollen abdomen. 'Charlie is going to be so worried.'

Abby gave a little smile at her pet name for her husband, the most important man in America, and gave her hand a squeeze. 'Has someone told your husband that you're here?'

Jennifer rolled her eyes in response. 'Oh, yes.'

Abby glanced over the notes Nancy was making of the foetal heart rate and the First Lady's blood pressure. Everything looked good.

'Don't worry, Jennifer. We'll take good care of you. I'm going to examine you in a few minutes to confirm that your waters have broken. Have you had any contractions at all?'

Jennifer shook her head. 'No, just the back pain. It's still there now.'

Nancy raised her eyebrow then moved quickly towards the door as it started to open. 'Yes, can I help you?' Her voice echoed around the room.

'Just to give you these, Mrs Taylor's medical records. Dr Storm said that you would need them.' A black-covered arm appeared through the tiny space in the doorway, brandishing a thick brown envelope, which Nancy snatched away before banging the door shut again.

Jennifer slumped back against her pillows. 'Poor Luke,' she murmured. 'I thought he was going to blow a gasket when he realised what was going on. I didn't know what else to do when Dr Blair started having chest pain—he seemed the most obvious person to call.' Her voice drifted off.

Abby felt as if she was missing something. 'How do you know Luke?'

'He's my husband's cardiologist.'

'The President has a cardiologist?'

'My husband has a doctor for everything—whether he needs it or not.' Jennifer gave a wry smile.

Abby gazed in wonder at the most watched woman in America. She might be the First Lady but she was still a first-time mom-to-be, who was probably just as worried as every other potential mother in the whole world. Her waters had broken early and the first thing she'd done had been to phone a doctor for the man having chest pain. She hadn't thought of herself first at all. This was some woman.

Abby gave a nod and slid the notes out from inside the envelope. 'I'll have a quick check over these and give our local obstetrician a call.' She moved towards the door. 'Nancy will stay with you for now and I'll be back in five minutes.'

She stepped outside and directly into the path of six black-suited men. They seemed to be multiplying by the minute. 'Excuse me,' she said, sidestepping them and heading over to the nearby desk.

She bent over to pick up the phone but was stopped as a firm bronzed hand slid in front of hers, picking up the phone first.

'Hey!'

Luke shot her a dazzling smile. All white teeth and tanned skin. Just the way she liked him. Just the way she remembered him. More little sparks fired inside her, sending a feeling to the pit of her stomach like…like what? It had been so long she couldn't remember.

'Sorry, Abby, I'm first. I need to take Dr Blair to the cath lab. He's a definite inferior MI.' He waved the ECG under her nose. 'Look at the ST elevation.' Then he paused for a second, the smile draining from his face. 'You do have cath-lab facilities, don't you?'

Abby nodded as a look of relief swept visibly over his face. 'Wait a minute, though, Luke. You've just come from Washington DC—you won't have a licence to practise medicine here.' Her brow furrowed. 'Or is there some crazy dispensation for the President's staff I don't know about?'

He raised his eyebrow as the corner of his mouth turned upwards. 'Yes and no. I can treat the President, but only the President, in any state. However, here...' he swept his arm outwards '...I've just been lucky. I've been working with two of California's universities and needed a licence to practise in the state. So don't worry, Abby, I'm covered.'

She gave a little nod. 'Just dial 032 and tell them what you've got. One of our nurse practitioners will monitor the patient for you and I'll get one of the residents to come and assist you with the procedure.'

'Will there be any issues with your own cardiologist?'

'Absolutely not. Our own cardiologist is currently thirty-eight weeks pregnant and has a full clinic this morning.' She gave a wave of her hand. 'I'll speak to her, you don't need to worry.' She listened while he finished the call, glancing over the medical records in front of her. Everything seemed good: no underlying conditions; no obvious problems with the baby. All antenatal care meticulously charted. Dr Blair was obviously no slouch—but then, this was the President's baby.

She reached over to grab the receiver as he hung up, her hand brushing against his. A delicious little zing shot up her arm. One that she hadn't felt in— how long? He must have felt it too as their eyes locked. And Abby stayed there. Frozen in that second in time. A whirlwind of electric memories all came back instantly—the long, lazy afternoons they'd spent together, the easy, comfortable relationship that they'd had together, the times when they'd both opened their mouths to speak and both said the same thing simultaneously, and the long, hot nights they'd spent locked in each other's arms. In that instant she was twenty-four again, her long blonde hair blowing in the wind as they'd stood at the top of the hill in Washington and he'd promised that he would stay with her for ever. A promise that had soon been broken. Broken on that same hill only a few months later. A promise that had broken her heart and sent her tumbling into an abyss.

But time had passed now. Time that appeared to have etched a few fine lines into Luke's forehead, making him seem older and maybe a little more careworn.

'Hello? Hello? Is someone there?'

Abby jolted from the daydream she'd been hiding in and stared at the phone receiver in her hand. She'd dialled the number automatically without even realising that she'd done it.

'Hi, David, it's Abby Tyler here. I've got a bit of an obstetric emergency. I wondered if you would mind coming in for a consult?'

A smile danced across her lips as she listened to the voice at the end of the phone. She could sense Luke's eyes on her, willing her not to say anything that would reveal the identity of their patient.

'Ten minutes would be great. Thanks, David.'

She replaced the phone and grinned. 'That's our emergency obstetrician. He'll be here soon.'

Luke leaned back against the nearby wall and folded his arms across his wide chest. His brow furrowed suspiciously. 'Why do I get the feeling you're not telling me something, Abby?'

She shook her head and winked at him. 'You'll see.'

A wave of fear swept across Luke's chest. 'No funny stuff, Abby. He's definitely an obstetrician?'

'Oh, yes, he's definitely an obstetrician.' One of the nearby nurse practitioners walked up quickly and touched Luke's arm.

'Dr Storm?'

He nodded swiftly.

'We'll be set up for you in the next ten minutes, I'm just going to get the patient.' She nodded towards Abby. 'Dr Tyler will tell you where we are.' She carried on down the corridor and into the trauma room to collect Dr Blair.

'Some things never change.' Abby surveyed the surrounding chaos around her. Her once peaceful emergency department looked as if it had been invaded by a black-suited army.

'What?' Luke glanced around him.

'Storm by name, Storm by nature.'

'You know I hate it when you say that.'

'That makes it all the more fun.' She watched as one black-suited man talked into his jacket lapel, while holding his finger to his ear, as if listening for a reply. She raised her eyebrow at Luke. 'We still have a problem here, Luke.'

'What do you mean?' The last thing he needed was more problems.

'I'm a paediatrician. I do children—kids.' She wiggled her hand in the air. 'I do some babies but certainly not *early* babies. Not neonates. We might have an obstetrician but what we really need is a neonatologist. And I'm not that.' She shook her head. 'This really isn't my specialty.'

Luke folded his arms across his chest. 'I've never known you to run from a challenge.'

Abby waved her hand around her. 'In an emergency situation I could probably muddle through. But if the baby needs supported ventilation then we just don't have the facilities, and this *is* the President's baby, Luke.'

'I know that.' He ran his fingers through his hair in exasperation. 'Well, what the hell are you doing here? Mendocino Valley, of all places?' His arm swept outwards across the expanse of the department.

Abby was instantly irritated. 'What do you mean by that?'

Luke tilted his head. 'Last time I saw you, you had just been offered the job of a lifetime in San Francisco. Five years later I find you here, in some backwater clinic in the middle of nowhere. What happened, Abby?'

Abby shook her head and carefully closed the notes in front of her, bringing them up and clutching them to her chest. 'Just shows how little you really knew me, Luke. It might well have been the job of a lifetime, but it wasn't *my* job of a lifetime. You happened, Luke. You made me re-evaluate my life. And even though I didn't think it at the time, you probably did me a favour. I love being

here in Mendocino Valley. I do still work in San
Francisco, but I only took the job because it means
I can work here, in Pelican Cove, for twelve weeks
a year. This is where I want to be.'

Luke's cool eyes watched her carefully, a wave
of guilt sweeping over him. For the second time
in five minutes he wondered what she wasn't telling him. She was holding the case notes to her
chest as if she were protecting a closely guarded
secret. The Abby Tyler he'd known had had the
world at her feet. She'd been approached by three
prestigious university hospitals to take part in their
paediatric residency programmes. She'd been dedicated and focused. Something about this wasn't
quite right. Why would the woman who'd been
top of her class and had had the pick of any job
be working in a backwater place like this?

CHAPTER TWO

ABBY watched with a sinking feeling in her heart as the nitrazine paper turned the tell-tale shade of blue. She raised her head and gave Jennifer a rueful smile as she showed her the paper. 'Well, I think we can safely say that your membranes have ruptured.'

'They have?'

'Yes. This paper turns blue when it comes into contact with amniotic fluid.'

Jennifer blew out a long, slow breath from her pursed lips. 'It's too early. What happens now?'

Abby snapped off her gloves, walking quickly to the sink to wash her hands. She finished and sat down at the side of the bed next to Jennifer, trying to work out what to tell her.

'It won't really be up to me, it will be up to Dr Fairgreaves—the obstetrician that's coming to see you. I just needed to confirm your membranes had ruptured so I can give him the whole picture.'

'Do you need to examine me any further?' Jennifer gave a little grimace and Abby knew exactly what she meant.

She shook her head. 'No, actually, that wouldn't be a good idea right now. Ideally what we want to do right now is to delay you going into labour for as long as possible.'

'Tell it to me straight, Dr Tyler.'

Abby leaned over and held Jennifer's hand. 'There are a number of things for Dr Fairgreaves to consider.' She held up the buff-coloured folder. 'From your notes I see that you're currently 31 weeks and 4 days. He may decide to give you some steroids to help mature your baby's lungs in case of early delivery. He might also decide to give you some antibiotics to help prevent infection.'

'Am I going to deliver early?'

Abby shook her head. 'I'm not really qualified to tell you that. I do know that about 80 per cent of women whose membranes rupture go into labour within four days.'

Jennifer took a deep breath and her hands rested automatically on her swollen abdomen. 'What are my baby's chances?'

Abby shook her head. 'We'll talk about that

when Dr Fairgreaves gets here. I want to hear what his professional opinion is before we start leaping to any conclusions. From right now, though, you're on strict bed rest.'

Jennifer threw up her hands in frustration. 'But I've already been on bed rest!'

Abby raised one eyebrow. 'Have you?'

Jennifer watched her carefully before finally answering, 'Well, maybe not *complete* bed rest.'

'We need to monitor your baby for any signs of distress and monitor you for any sign of infection.' She hesitated a little before continuing, 'It might also be advisable to move you to a hospital with better facilities for pre-term babies.'

Jennifer looked deep in thought and bit her bottom lip. 'Where would that be?'

'The nearest is San Francisco Children's Hospital. They have a special ICU for premature deliveries.'

'No.'

The voice was clear and decisive and took Abby completely by surprise.

'What?'

Jennifer folded her arms firmly across her chest. 'I'm staying here.'

Abby shook her head in disbelief. 'Why on earth would you want to stay here?'

'Wouldn't moving me be dangerous?'

Abby shifted uncomfortably. Jennifer's sharp retort unnerved her. In an instant she was in a witness box and being cross-examined by the more-than-capable lawyer. This wasn't her specialty and she was beginning to feel at little out of her depth. 'This is a conversation you need to have with your obstetrician.'

'Oh.'

This response was different. Quiet and unsure. She'd gone from being a feisty lawyer to an imminent first-time mom in a matter of seconds. This woman was more scared than she was letting on.

'What's he like?' Jennifer ran her fingers through her uncombed hair. 'Your obstetrician.' She hesitated for a second. 'Is he good?'

Abby gave her a little smile. 'Officially he's retired. But in answer to your question he's better than good—he's great.' She was interrupted by a heavy knock at the door.

'Abby…Dr Tyler, can I see you please?'

Abby could hear the anxiety in Luke's voice.

She gave Jennifer a smile, picked up the notes and headed to the door. 'I'll be back in a few minutes.'

She pulled a pen from her pocket as she opened the door. She wanted to make sure she'd recorded everything perfectly. With her head in the notes she walked straight into Luke's broad chest.

'Ow! Luke, what are you doing?'

Luke shook his head and pointed sideways in exasperation. 'Please tell me that isn't your obstetrician.'

Abby followed to where his finger was pointing to a small dishevelled character dressed from head to toe in fishing gear, with an upright fishing rod perched precariously in his hand. He was surrounded on all sides by men in black suits and was protesting loudly, 'Who the hell are you lot?'

Abby's face broke into a wide smile. 'It certainly is,' she said as she shouldered her way past the security detail. 'Dr Fairgreaves, I'm so glad you're here.' She wrapped him in a warm embrace and pulled him to one side. 'We need to have a private chat about our patient.'

She handed him the buff-coloured folder and watched as he ran his eyes over the presidential seal on the bottom corner of the notes. His eyes narrowed. 'Who's this?' He gestured in frustration as a figure appeared at Abby's side.

Luke. 'I was just about to ask you the same question,' he muttered under his breath.

'I might be old, son, but there's nothing wrong with my hearing.'

'Well, do you always come to work looking like this?' Luke gestured towards the fishing gear.

'Son, I try not to come to work at all if I can help it. I'm retired.'

'You're retired?' Luke's voice rose in pitch.

Abby cleared her throat loudly before the conversation got out of hand. 'Luke, I'd like you to meet Dr David Fairgreaves, our honorary obstetrician, and, David, I'd like you to meet Dr Luke Storm, he's a cardiologist from Washington who brought the First Lady in.'

David's brow furrowed in confusion. 'Why the hell is a cardiologist bringing a pregnant lady to hospital?'

Abby smiled. In an instant she wasn't the First Lady any more, she was simply an expectant mother, like any other. She loved that about David Fairgreaves—even though he'd been pursued by many dignitaries and celebrities for his services, he never wasted time on pomp and ceremony. His patients were just that, *his patients.*

Abby slid her arm around David Fairgreaves's shoulders, 'Her own obstetrician is currently having an MI—Luke is about to treat him.'

David stared at Luke for a moment before finally grunting, 'Fine, then.' He sat down and started reading the notes.

Luke stood frozen to the spot. 'David Fairgreaves? *The* David Fairgreaves?'

Abby nodded in recognition of the man who was famous all over America for his ground-breaking work. He'd received numerous awards for pioneering the procedure to retrieve stem cells from the umbilical cord. Something that seemed almost commonplace now, but at the time had been a real revolutionary leap of faith. He'd done that while continuing to work as an obstetrician and was known as one of the best in America.

Luke groaned. 'This is turning into a bad TV show. What on earth is David Fairgreaves doing here?'

'You mean in this backwater place?' She couldn't help the sarcasm that crept into her voice. Then, seeing the expression on his face, Abby sneaked her hand around his waist and gave him a quick hug. Luke's stress levels seemed to be going through the roof. The warmth of his body immediately poured through her skin. She raised her head up towards his and smiled. 'Fishing.'

'What?' Luke looked totally bewildered.

She shrugged her shoulders. 'He's got a fishing boat in Pelican Cove, and now he's retired he spends half the year here. We have an informal arrangement together that I can call him out for any obstetric emergencies and he loves it.'

Luke studied the man in the rumpled clothes sitting in the chair in front of him. 'He looks about a hundred and ten,' he whispered.

'Well, he's not quite that old,' she whispered back, 'and he's as sharp as a tack so don't annoy him.'

Luke looked as if he could spontaneously combust at any second. Abby pulled her arm from his waist and turned to face him, taking both his hands in hers.

'Look on the bright side, Luke. If someone had asked you to pick any doctor in the world to deliver the President's pre-term baby, who would you have picked?'

She watched as the significance of her words began to sink in. The deep wrinkles in Luke's forehead began to soften. 'I guess you're right,' he said.

'You know I am.' She lifted herself up on her tip toes and kissed the tip of his nose. 'Now, go and deal with your MI. I'll come and find you if there's any problems.'

He nodded, still lost in thought, before taking a deep breath and pulling his hands from hers. 'Okay,' he murmured as he turned and started to head off down the corridor.

Abby watched for a second. Her lips felt as if they were on fire. A thousand little pins were prickling them, leaving them alive with sensation after touching his skin.

'Dr Tyler?'

Abby started at the deep voice behind her.

'Yes?'

'I'm James Turner.' He held out his hand towards her. 'I'm in charge of the protective detail for the First Lady.'

Abby nodded silently. The craggy-faced man from earlier. He was a large, imposing fellow with a small scar that snaked across the bridge of his nose. Her mind exploded with a thousand possibilities as to how it had got there, before his intense gaze jerked her back into focus. 'Sorry,' she muttered. 'What can I do for you, Mr Turner?'

'This is your department?' It didn't sound like a question coming from his lips, more like a statement.

'Yes, it is.'

'Well, sorry, ma'am, but I need to close your emergency department down.'

'What?' Abby's screech of disbelief echoed around the building. 'You most certainly will not. I won't let you. You don't have the authority to do that…'

He silenced her by holding his hand up directly in front of her face.

'I do have the authority. As of now, your department is closed. I also need access to all your personnel files.'

'What?' This was just going from bad to worse. He wanted to close her department and then spend the day looking at files?

'I need to have access to everyone's history. We need to run security checks on everyone in the building.'

'You want to do what? No! You can't do that!'

'Yes, yes, I can. And I will.' His broad hand had caught her arm to stop her gesticulating wildly. 'Nothing is more important than the safety and security of the First Lady.'

Abby took a deep breath. 'Look, Mr Turner, while I appreciate you have a job to do—so do I. This is a small community.' She waved her arm around the department. 'I know every single member of staff here. None of them are a risk to the First Lady's safety or security. I can personally vouch for them all.'

'That's very nice, Dr Tyler.' He shot her a white-toothed, crooked grin. 'But it's not going to cut it. We'll run our own checks on everyone here.' He glanced around the bustling department. 'And we're going to have to restrict the number of staff.'

Abby shook her head. 'This is a community hospital, Mr Turner. We serve a widespread population that doesn't have easy access to emergency facilities. If you close us down, the nearest emergency unit is 50 miles away. If there's an accident at one of the nearby saw mills, or at the harbour, that travel time could cost the life of a patient. We also have links with a special-needs school near here—Parkside. We often have children brought in with breathing or feeding difficulties—taking them somewhere else would cause immense difficulties.'

She glanced towards the white board, which only showed three patients in the department at the moment—two of whom were with James Turner. 'We're not normally this quiet.' Her mind was spinning with endless possibilities. 'I know this isn't an ideal situation but the most realistic solution is to move Jennifer Taylor to one of the ward areas once Dr Fairgreaves has examined her. If she's out of the emergency department, do you really have to close us down?' Abby couldn't keep the pleading sound out of her voice. She just couldn't turn patients away, not when they needed her. 'I'll let you see the personnel records if you want—just let me check with the hospital administrator. You're not going to find anything anyway, but please don't close down the emergency department.'

'Do you have floor plans for the hospital?'

He hadn't moved a muscle. Abby was sure he hadn't even blinked.

'What? Yes...yes, I think so.' She pointed over

his shoulder. 'They'll be in the hospital administrator's office.'

'I'll get back to you, Dr Tyler.' He turned swiftly
on his heel and stalked off in the direction of the
nearby office.

Abby leaned back against the nearby wall and
breathed a huge sigh of relief. There was only one
other patient in the department right now. Dr Fairgreaves was dealing with Jennifer Taylor. She'd
need to wait and see what his recommendations
would be. She glanced at her watch and stared up
the corridor. She could almost feel the invisible
pull. Luke was up there. Probably performing an
angioplasty. It had been years since she'd seen him
at work. Maybe it was time to go and offer some
moral support?

Luke's head was spinning. He pushed open the
door to the changing room with unexpected venom
and started as it thumped off the wall. The First
Lady was going to have her baby. Her obstetrician
had had an MI. The new obstetrician looked like a
tramp but had the credentials of a king. And they
were stuck in some backwater part of Mendocino

Valley. Stuck with Abby Tyler. He couldn't have made this up.

He tugged at his red tie and undid the buttons on his shirt, stuffing them in a nearby empty locker. Behind him he found a variety of sizes of theatre scrubs and pulled the familiar clothing over his head.

And she'd kissed him. The lightest kiss, as if a feather had brushed the tip of his nose, and it had sent his blood soaring through his veins as if a rocket had just taken off. What on earth was happening? They'd laughed through their medical training together, stressed through their exams, but spent most of their time in each other's arms. And for a while he had never been happier. The dark cloud that had hung over his head since his brother had died had finally lifted. He'd met the woman of his dreams. The woman he wanted to spend the rest of his life with. Until she'd started to talk about the future. *Their* future. A future that involved them having a family. And the dark cloud had appeared again, nestling around his head and shoulders until it had completely enveloped him.

They had been midway through their specialist training by then—he in cardiology, she in paediatrics. And he'd begun to see her in a completely different light. Whenever she'd spoken about the kids, even the ones with terrible outcomes, she'd had a sparkle in her eyes. On the few occasions he'd gone to pick her up from the ward, he'd never found her stuck in an office with her head in the notes—no, she had always been right in the middle of things, leading the games in the middle of the ward, usually with a child under each arm.

He'd seen a few of his friends start to flourish when they'd commenced their specialty, becoming more animated and enthusiastic when they'd spoken about their work. But Abby had truly blossomed. She had excelled at her job and hadn't hidden her thrill at finally specialising in paediatrics. And after years of study that's when she'd started to plan ahead. To plan for a family. A family he could never have. And that's when he'd broken her heart. That's when he told her he was infertile—an unfortunate complication of teenage mumps.

There had been so many other things going on in his life at the time, and although he had known it was important, he hadn't taken the time or had the maturity to understand the wider implications—

that one day he would meet the woman of his dreams and she would want a family. A family he couldn't give her.

Maybe it was his fault? Maybe he should have told her right from the beginning that he couldn't have kids. But then again, it wasn't your everyday normal topic of conversation. But three years into their relationship—when he'd started to see the signs—he'd sat her down and told her.

To give her her due, Abby had made all the right noises, told him it didn't matter, that she loved him and that they would find a way to have a family together. But for Luke it had been the death knell of their relationship.

From the moment he'd heard the word 'infertile' he'd blocked out all thoughts of a family. Surely there was a hidden message there? If he couldn't have kids naturally, maybe he wasn't meant to have kids?

She'd talked about donor sperm, adoption, other possibilities—but he hadn't wanted to think about those options. Truth was he wasn't ready to consider those options as he hadn't really faced up to his infertility yet. So he'd shut himself off from those conversations and had point-blank refused to consider any possibilities.

Every time after that he'd looked at Abby, he'd felt as if he was cheating her. Cheating her out of the opportunity to be a mother.

Five years they'd been together but they'd slowly, but surely, drifted apart.

The door on the other side leading into the theatre swung open. 'Dr Storm?' A pretty Asian woman looked at him, her dark hair poking out from under a theatre cap. He nodded.

She stuck out her hand. 'Good, I'm Dr Lydia King. Abby sent me along to assist you.' He gave her a little nod in recognition as he shook her hand and she backed out the door again. 'I'll just check on the patient and see you in there.'

A wave of anticipation swept over Luke as he pushed open the doors and entered the cardiac cath lab, quickly followed by a wave of nausea, most likely because he hadn't had a chance to eat yet today. He glanced about him quickly, taking in the layout and equipment available. One of the NPs appeared at his side. 'We're all set up for you.' She pointed in the direction of the sinks. 'You can scrub up over there and I'll gown you up. Would you like to come over and speak to Dr Blair first?'

Luke gave her a quick smile. 'Of course I would.' It only took three strides to cross over to where Dr Blair was lying on the table, monitors attached, pale and sweaty. 'How's Jennifer?' he gasped.

Luke gave him a quick pat on the shoulder. 'She's just being examined now by one of the obstetricians but she's doing fine. Let's worry about you first.'

He watched the rapid, shallow breaths. 'Let me explain the procedure to you.'

Dr Blair waved his hand in the air. 'Son, don't teach an old dog new tricks, just stick the thing in and get this blockage cleared. I feel as if a train is sitting on my chest,' he wheezed.

Luke nodded. 'Give me a few minutes while I scrub up and I'll talk to you while we're doing the procedure.' He cast his eyes over one of the nearby monitors. 'Can Dr Blair have some oxygen, please?'

The NP nodded before pulling a mask over Dr Blair's head. She followed Luke over to the sink and waited while he scrubbed up. The door open and he turned as Abby came in.

'Hi, Luke. You don't mind a spectator, do you? I don't get the chance to come in here much.'

Luke shook his head and shot her a gleaming smile from beneath his blue theatre hat. 'Of course I don't, Abby, you're welcome in my cath lab any time.'

The words sent a shiver running down Abby's spine and she felt a little warmth in her cheeks as she looked anxiously around the room. Had anyone else noticed? No, everyone else was going about their daily business. No one had noticed a thing. Maybe it was all in her mind?

And then he began. And it was like watching a master at work.

'Are we ready to start?' Luke asked Lydia and she gave him a quick nod as she finished administering the sedative.

'Okay, Dr Blair, I'm just going to insert a little local anaesthetic down here.' Abby watched as Luke swabbed the groin area surrounded by surgical drapes then numbed the area with local anaesthetic. He waited a few moments before lifting a scalpel and making a small nick into the skin, then expertly inserted the sheath into the artery.

With slow and deliberate actions he watched the

X-ray monitor carefully as he slowly guided the catheter into place until it reached the site of the blockage. Over the course of the next 30 minutes he inserted the contrast material and established the full extent of the blockage.

'Okay, Dr Blair, there is quite a significant blockage in your artery so I'm going to insert a stent to ensure we keep your artery open.' He turned his head and exchanged a few words with Lydia, who gave him a nod in approval.

'I'm going to use one of the newer drug-eluting stents. Have you heard of them?'

Dr Blair gave a little shake of his head from the theatre table.

'This type of stent is coated with a medication that is slowly released to help keep the blood vessel from re-narrowing. They've just recently been approved for clinical use in the coronary arteries and I've had some really favourable results when I've used them.'

'Whatever you think, Doc.' Dr Blair waved his hand in nonchalance from the effect of the sedatives.

Luke gave a little smile and continued. Abby watched from the sidelines. He was an entirely different character in here. In his familiar medical setting Luke was the calmest man in the room. The consummate professional, who was relaxed and happy in his field of expertise. She almost laughed. She'd forgotten just how good he was. But take him out of his expert field…

A smile danced across her lips as she remembered the look on his face when he'd entered her emergency room—with his furrowed brow and anxiety levels reaching skyward. Not to mention when he'd first set eyes on Dr Fairgreaves in his fishing gear. She'd thought at that point he was going to blow a gasket at the thought of some country bumpkin delivering the President's baby. But in here he was cool, calm and collected. None of the previous worries or anxieties showed. She watched as he spoke quietly to his surrounding staff, expertly guiding the stent into place, before removing the guide wire and catheter and applying firm pressure on the site.

He stood there for ten minutes, continuing to reinforce to Dr Blair what he'd done and giving instructions on follow-up care to the staff. 'Can we keep him flat initially, please, and monitor the catheter site for bleeding and swelling? You can give me a call if there are any problems.' He looked over his shoulder. 'Abby, do you have an emergency page you can give me in the meantime?'

Abby lifted her hand to show the pager she was already holding in her hand. 'Your wish is my command.' She laughed. 'Just as well I switched my telepathic powers on this morning.' She turned to the other staff. 'You'll be able to page Dr Storm on 556. If you forget, I've given his details to the switchboard operator.' She turned back to Luke, just as his stomach let out a loud rumble. 'Come on, I'll wait with you while you change. I think it's about time we had a coffee.'

Music to his ears. This was the weirdest day in history. Luke smiled as he held open the door for her. Thank the Lord for mixed changing rooms. Abby walked in front of him and his eyes fixated on her butt. She was wearing the same thin green scrubs he was, but on her they seemed so much more alluring. He squinted, trying to see through them. Where was her VPL? There was none. What did that mean? He felt a rush of blood. Thank the Lord that no one else was in here. 'Do you do killer-strength coffee here?'

She raised her eyebrow. 'In this backwater town? Do you still take four shots in one cup?'

The door banged shut behind them and he caught her by the waist and spun her around. 'What do you think?'

Through the thin scrubs that she was wearing he could feel the warmth of her skin. Her head was just below his chin and there was that strawberry lip gloss again. Invading his senses and making every hair on his body stand on end. He gave out a little involuntary groan as she stepped closer, pressing her body against his. To hell with decorum. There had been too many distractions today already.

'I think my telepathic powers are still working,' she whispered, fixing him with her deep brown eyes. 'And you're not thinking about coffee any more.'

'Five years is a long time, Abby,' he growled.

'Five years is a *very* long time, Luke.'

It was all the indication he needed. His hands crept around the edges of her waist, pulling her even closer, pressing her firm breasts against his muscled chest. Her head was tilted upwards towards his. Her eyes already half-shut, lips slightly parted in readiness for his kiss.

Using all the restraint he could muster, he bent his head and kissed her lightly, slowly, his teeth brushing her bottom lip. Her hands slid up around his neck, pulling him even closer. This was heaven. Heaven that he hadn't known in five years.

The kiss grew deeper, more passionate, bringing with it the most natural, primal response. This would be the time in the movie that the romantic music started playing and they both fell to the floor in the bedroom of the beach house, with the patio doors wide open to the beach, a tropical sunset and waves lapping up towards them. But it wasn't.

Right now all he wanted to do was have her. Right here. Right now. On the changing-room floor. Up against the wall. He didn't care.

He slid his hand inside her scrub trousers. Bare skin. He almost groaned out loud. Then his fingers caught it, the edge of her thong. Abby in a thong. Now, there was a sight he hadn't seen in years. His fingers flicked a little lower and she let out a gasp.

It stopped him in his tracks. Luke stepped back

reluctantly, releasing her from his grasp, knowing that at any moment anyone could walk through either of the changing-room doors.

'Abby…'

'Don't. Don't say anything, Luke.' Her breathing was hard and ragged. She adjusted her scrub top, which had ridden up past her waist, pulling it down sharply to reveal her erect nipples, clearly visible through the thin fabric.

His eyes fixated on the view, causing her to look down and cross her arms in front of her chest in embarrassment. 'Stop it.'

'I wasn't doing anything.' The corners of his lips turned upwards in the beginnings of a smile.

Abby sat down on the nearby bench and put her head in her hands. 'This is madness.'

Luke hovered for an instant, unsure of what to do next, before sitting down next to her. His thigh brushed against hers and she jerked her leg away.

Her fingers parted slightly and she peeked out at him. 'Stop touching me.'

He raised his eyebrow. 'I am not having a conversation with a pair of hands.'

'You're going to have to, because I can't stand looking at you.'

'No, I'm not.' His broad hands enveloped hers and gently pulled them away from her flushed face. 'We're adults, Abby, not children.'

'You're making me feel as if I'm eighteen again.'

Laughter lines appeared all around his eyes as a huge smile took over his face. He leaned forward and whispered in her ear, 'Now, that I really *would* like to see again.'

She swatted at his leg as a new wash of red swept up into her cheeks. 'Stop it. No, I mean it, stop it.'

Luke leaned back against the wall, folding his arms across his chest as he watched her babble. He was amused. The unflappable Abby Tyler was flustered. This was twice in one day. Had he ever seen her this way before?

She stood up and started pacing across the room. 'You've got a lot of nerve, you know? Coming in here with the First Lady, *the First Lady* no less, and wreaking havoc in my emergency room. And as for the black brigade—they seem to have an amazing ability to self-replicate—they're like a virus. One minute there's five of them, two minutes later there's ten of them! Where do they come from?' She threw her hands in the air in exasperation. 'And James Turner—the Man in Black—threatened to shut my emergency department! And do you know they're checking the personnel files of all my staff? How dare they? Bursting in here, taking over the place, then checking on my staff, *my staff*! Who do they think they are?' Her voice had reached fever pitch by now.

Abby was frustrated. She was *beyond* frustrated. Sexually frustrated. Something she hadn't experienced in five years. She'd just gone from the starting blocks to practically the finishing line in the flicker of an eye. Or more like the flicker of a finger.

But this wasn't her. She didn't do things like this any more. So why were her legs like jelly? Why couldn't she look him in the eye? And why was she ranting and raving like an idiot? Things had changed. She couldn't do anything like this now.

'Have you finished?'

'Hell, no! And as for you...' She pointed a finger at him accusingly. 'You virtually disappeared off the planet. No nice emails, no phone calls. Then you come in here after all this time and kiss me! Kiss me as if we've never been apart.' *And please kiss me again, only this time don't stop.* 'I don't know what you've been doing for the last five years, or where you've been, or who you've been with.' Her voice fell as a sudden realisation hit her. 'You could be married for all I know.' Her eyes fell automatically to his left hand. No ring. Her eyes met his. 'Are you?'

Luke shook his head. In an instant the colour had left her face, leaving her deathly pale. She looked as if she could fall over. He stood up and caught her by the shoulders. 'Abby, calm down.' He shook his head. 'I'm not married—of course I'm not married—I wouldn't be kissing you if I was.'

The words hung in the air. He lifted his finger and touched her cheek. 'And you know why there were no phone calls, no emails. Not because I didn't care, Abby. I cared *too* much. And we both had to move on. I couldn't do that if I'd seen or spoken to you every day—and it looks like you couldn't too. You moved here, remember?'

She looked stunned. He was touching her again and the heat from his body was electric, causing ripple effects all over again. She shrugged her shoulders out from under his grasp. 'I told you to stop touching me,' she muttered as she turned around and started pulling things from the locker in front of her. 'Here, put your clothes back on, please.' She shoved his trousers at him, her hands feeling the expensive fabric beneath her fingers. 'I guess you didn't buy these in Target, did you?'

Her eyes fell to the obvious lump in his scrubs. It was still there. It hadn't disappeared in an instant. After all this time she could still have a long-lasting effect on him. Was that good or bad? 'Well, hurry up and put them on, maybe they'll give you a little more coverage.' She turned and pulled out his now crumpled white shirt and silk red tie, glancing at the labels. 'You must be Washington's best-dressed doctor.'

Luke shook his head and grabbed the shirt out of her hands, dropping it on the bench next to him as he pulled his scrub top over his head.

Abby stood frozen to the spot. The last time she'd seen those sun-kissed pecs and abs she'd been all over them. There was something really disconcerting about standing in an enclosed space with a half-dressed man who'd just kissed you. And his cheeky grin was infuriating her. No, *really* infuriating her.

This was all just a joke to him. He didn't know

how much her stomach was churning. She didn't even care that the First Lady and her SWOT team were there. Well, maybe that wasn't strictly true. But the First Lady was a patient, and patients she could deal with. Ex-lovers who'd broken her heart she couldn't. Especially when they looked like Luke. With his white-blond hair, tanned skin and gleaming teeth he looked as if any minute now an ad company would come running in with their cameras, strap a surfboard to his back and whizz him off to an exotic beach location somewhere for a photo shoot.

She watched as he turned slightly to put his arm in his sleeve. Her breath caught in her throat as she saw something new, a little zigzag scar running across his shoulder blade. Before she had time to even think about it her finger was touching it.

'That's new. What happened?'

He stopped, leaving his shirt hanging halfway down his back as the tip of her finger lightly traced the line of the scar. 'Abby…'

'What?' She was mesmerised by the ragged, up-lifted skin. Maybe Luke wasn't so perfect, after all?

Luke took a deep breath and glanced downwards. 'Stop touching me,' he growled.

She followed his gaze and pulled her hand back sharply. 'Oops, sorry.' She took a few steps and flattened herself against the far wall. She couldn't touch him from over there. Just as well. She averted her eyes as he stepped out of the flimsy scrubs and into his designer trousers. Well, she tried to move her gaze, but still happened to catch the slightest glimpse of his trademark white tight-fitting shorts. Shorts that left nothing to the imagination, causing her to feel a tingling sensation between her thighs.

'You're driving me crazy,' he growled again.

'Sorry.' She turned her back and found herself staring at the wall. Great. She was trapped in an enclosed space with a man she hadn't seen in five years and all she wanted to do was jump on him. Now she really was acting like a teenager. Who was this Abby Tyler? Time to change the subject.

'So how did you get the job?'

'What job?'

'Working for the President, of course!'

'Oh, that job.' She heard him rustling for a moment. 'You can turn around now.'

Could she? Would he be completely undressed and ready for her? She whipped around. There he was. Fully dressed and still looking good enough to eat. She almost gave a sigh of disappointment. 'Straighten your tie,' she said as she pointed at the crooked tie. 'I'd do it for you but I'm not allowed to touch.'

He gave her a sarcastic smile as he straightened his tie. 'I don't really work for the President. I'm just on his list.'

'What does that mean—on his list?'

Luke shrugged his shoulders. 'I think they just like to cover all eventualities. I was approached a few years ago and asked if I would be the President's cardiologist. They ran a huge number of checks on me, with my permission of course, and after a few months came back and explained that they would call if I was needed.'

'I thought all the President's doctors were from the military?'

Luke shrugged his shoulders. 'They usually are. But the military doesn't cover all areas. The President's physician is from the military and he's in charge of the White House medical unit. But some of the other specialists are like me—just called in when, and if, they're needed. Dr Blair was Jennifer Taylor's family obstetrician. She brought him with her, because it's been a long time since the White House needed an obstetrician.'

'So you've never actually met him?'

Luke shook his head. 'No, and today was the first time I'd met the First Lady too.'

'And here was me thinking that you were their best friend! I guess it didn't hurt that you were connected?'

His face darkened. 'I'd like to think they contacted me because of my professional expertise, rather than the fact my father's a senator.'

Abby flinched. Well, that was one way to dampen the sexual tension in the room. She should have known better. Luke's relationship with his father was strained enough, without her insinuating that he'd been given an easy route into a prestigious position. She'd forgotten how much he prickled at the mere mention of his father. 'I'm sure they did.' She held open the nearby door, allowing some cool, fresh air into the claustrophobic changing room—just what they both needed—and resisting the temptation to look and see if the telltale bulge in his trousers was under control yet. 'Are you ready? Let's go and get you that four-shot coffee you wanted.'

'Actually, I'm not strictly a four-shot drinker any more. I've mellowed.'

Abby choked in disbelief at the words. 'You? Mellowed? Well, I never thought I'd see the day!'

He quirked an eyebrow at her. 'I might surprise you.'

He grabbed the door and fell into step beside her, his arm draping easily across her shoulders, like it was the most natural thing in the world. And it was.

She gave him a sideways smile. 'Luke?'

'Yeah?'

'We're going to have to have some rules about touching...'

CHAPTER THREE

THE canteen was small and informal, nothing like the chaotic and bustling university hospital canteen Luke was used to.

'Your usual, Abby?' the assistant called from behind the serving counter.

'Thanks, Jan.' She turned and looked at Luke. 'What would you like?'

Luke resisted the temptation to say what came to mind and looked around, puzzled. The place was immaculate but he couldn't exactly see what food was on offer. 'What's your usual?'

Abby gave a little smile and glanced at her watch. 'You probably expect me to have something healthy like fruit juice and an apple but, at this time of day, and because nine times out of ten I miss lunch, it's a latte and one of Jan's home-made pancakes.'

'Mmm, that sounds good. I'll have the same.'

'Make that two, Jan,' she shouted over her shoulder.

Luke stuck his hand in his pocket and pulled out some money as two steaming tall latte glasses appeared, followed by two plates with hot pancakes. His stomach growled loudly at the appetising aroma, reminding him how long it had been since he'd eaten.

Abby waved her arm. 'Put your money away— I've got a tab.' She lifted the tray and walked over to a nearby table, sitting down and handing him his latte glass and plate. The canteen was quiet, with only a few other people sitting at the surrounding tables.

Luke leaned over and took a deep breath. 'Mmm, this smells great. I haven't had home-made pancakes in years.'

Abby bit her lip. When they'd lived together as medical students home-made pancakes had been one of their Sunday-morning rituals, along with a number of other things… Luke obviously didn't remember. Maybe reliving the past wasn't as good as Abby thought it was.

He looked around him. Sunlight was streaming though the nearby window, which overlooked the lush green gardens. The canteen was at the back of the hospital, facing onto the hills. The garden beds were packed with brightly coloured flowers and obviously well tended. The bushes were shaped and trimmed into neat round circles. So instead of feeling deprived of the ocean view, this really was a little piece of paradise.

'So how long have you worked here, Abby?'

She took a sip of her coffee. 'For the last five years. I was lucky, I was able to transfer from Washington to San Francisco on my residency programme. And when I got here, the programme included covering shifts down here. They never needed to ask me twice. Once I was qualified, the paediatrician post came up that included coverage down here and I leapt at the chance.'

Luke nodded. Things started slotting into place. She'd transferred almost immediately after they'd broken up. It wasn't easy to swap residency programmes, so someone must have pulled some strings. He watched as Abby spread butter over her pancake.

'What, no syrup?'

She shook her head. 'My tastes have changed— just like yours.' She pointed to his coffee.

Luke blinked. What did she mean, her tastes had changed? Was that a dig at him? She hadn't kissed him as though her tastes had changed. She'd kissed him as though they'd never been apart. The silence in the air was heavy between them.

Luke opened his mouth to speak again but she interrupted him.

'So what have you been doing in Washington? I've seen your name on a couple of research papers.'

'You have?' His eyes lit up with genuine excitement. His job was his passion. But more than that, she'd obviously been keeping tabs on his work. Why would she do that if she wasn't interested? 'Well, you'll have seen I've helped in the development and clinical trials of one of the newer types of stents.'

She nodded in appreciation, her mouth now stuffed with pancake.

'I've also been doing some drug trials—some in kids with cardiac conditions. I've been working with a paediatrician called Lisa Jones. Do you know her?'

It was all she could do not to choke on her pancake. Abby nodded again. Oh, she knew her all right. Lisa Jones, paediatrician extraordinaire—or so you would believe if you spoke to her. 'Luscious

Lisa', her friends called her. Along with the motto *Never leave your man alone in a room with her.* Lisa did most of her best work in the horizontal position, especially around promotion time.

Her eyes were automatically drawn to Luke. With his blond hair, pale blue eyes and surfer-boy build and tan, he would be a prime target for Lisa. Something that made her feel physically sick. She pushed her pancake away.

'So what *exactly* has Lisa been doing for you?'

Luke raised his eyebrows at the tone in her voice. 'She's been identifying suitable candidates for the study,' he said pointedly. He bent forward and took a sip of his coffee. 'I can see you're obviously not in her fan club.'

'Show me a woman that is.'

He shook his head. 'She's actually really clever and has a good grasp of the research ethics and principles required for drug trials.'

'That's not all she usually has a good grasp of.'

Luke put down his glass, a smile creeping across his face. 'Abby, are you jealous?'

'Why on earth would I be jealous?' Right now she would cheerfully pull every one of Luscious Lisa's mahogany locks from her head if she had a chance. A fist tightened around her heart. What on earth was wrong with her? She hadn't seen Luke in five years—she had absolutely no right to feel jealous of any relationship he may, or may not, be having. So how come the thought of him playing bedroom hockey with Lisa Jones was driving her insane?

Luke shook his head and reached across the table for her hand. 'I've never seen you so riled up. You're usually so laid back you're horizontal.'

'Just like Lisa?' The words were out before she had time to think about them.

Her pager sounded loudly, causing both of them to jump. They'd been so caught up in each other that they'd almost forgotten about the situation surrounding them. Luke reluctantly released her hand.

Abby glanced down at the number on her pager attached to her scrubs. She stood up immediately, pushing the chair backwards with a screech. 'It's Dr Fairgreaves. He needs to speak to me now.'

Luke stood up, the tell-tale worry lines appearing on his brow instantly. 'Mind if I tag along?'

'Not at all.'

They headed out the doors towards the ER.

Abby couldn't shift the uncomfortable feeling in her gut. He hadn't exactly answered her question. What had Lisa Jones been doing for Luke? And why the hell couldn't she get thoughts of the two of them out of her mind?

Dr Fairgreaves was sitting in one of the two doctors' offices in the ER, writing furiously in the First Lady's notes. He was still wearing his dark green fishing hat over his unruly hair but had donned a more traditional white coat. He leaned back in his chair as Abby and Luke came into the small room.

'Do you want the good news or the bad news?'

They turned and looked at each other for a second, wondering what was coming next.

Dr Fairgreaves continued. 'The good news is that we don't have an immediate arrival. But we probably will have at some point in the next four days. The bad news is that she doesn't want to go back to Washington.'

'What?' Luke's voice went up about ten decibels.

'Oh, no,' Abby groaned, and held her head in her hands.

'What do you mean, she doesn't want to go back to Washington?'

Dr Fairgreaves smiled at Luke. 'She's quite some woman. I'd hate to be up against her in a court of law. I doubt I'd come out alive.'

'But that's ridiculous.' Luke looked around him. 'There are no facilities here for a premature baby. Maybe if she was thirty-six or thirty-seven weeks, but not at this stage.'

Abby sagged down in a nearby chair. 'I thought she was going to do this,' she said quietly.

Luke spun around to face her, his face incredulous. 'You knew? And you didn't tell me?'

Abby took a deep breath. 'She sort of mentioned it. I told her she'd have to discuss it with Dr Fairgreaves.' She turned to face him. 'Sorry, David.'

He gave a little smile. 'Not your fault.'

Luke broke in, 'This isn't safe. Not by a long shot. This might not be my specialty but I can't let this happen. No, *we* can't let this happen. What would normally happen in a case like this?'

David Fairgreaves took a deep breath, looking vaguely amused at how wound up Luke was becoming. 'Actually, you have more responsibility for this than you know. Is it safe to put your patient on a plane right now? Or subject him to a long road transfer?'

'What? Dr Blair? Of course not. He's had a significant MI, with angioplasty and stent insertion. He'll need to stay here for a few days. What's that got to do with the First Lady?'

'A lot, actually. She has a great deal of trust in Dr Blair. She doesn't want to leave him.'

'Even if that puts her baby at risk?'

'It doesn't have to.'

Luke looked stunned. 'What do you mean? Dr Blair is in no fit state to be consulting with the First Lady right now.'

'To answer your earlier question, we would normally transfer a lady in Jennifer Taylor's condition to San Francisco's Children and Maternity Hospital, where they have excellent neonatal facilities. However, from the First Lady's perspective, if she goes to San Francisco there will be a huge media circus. It's a big hospital—you couldn't possibly hope to contain the news that the First Lady was there, particularly when she's supposed to be in Washington. But here...' he pointed out the window at the magnificent ocean view '...we have a much better chance of containing the story.' He glanced down at the notes he had made. 'As the baby is still under thirty-two weeks, I've written her up for some steroids and some antibiotics. Nothing out of the ordinary and we'll monitor her.' He folded his arms across his chest. 'The health and well-being of my patient comes first. She's already under enough stress and I won't add to it.' He raised an eyebrow at Luke. 'And I won't let *you* add to it either.' He turned towards Abby and handed her a blank A4 notebook and pen. 'Make a list.'

'Of what?' Her mind was spinning. But she knew he was right. Dr Fairgreaves had seen past the words and bravado and seen a frightened mom-to-be.

'Everything you need. And *everybody* you need. Chances are we've got between one and four days to plan for this delivery.'

'Are you joking?'

'No. I'm deadly serious.' He waved his arms. 'It might not be an ideal situation but we can make this a safe environment for the President's baby to be born in. All we need is the staff and the equipment. It's only people and things. Moveable objects. Who is the best neonatologist that you know?'

'Lincoln Adams at San Fran.' The name rolled off Abby's tongue without a moment's hesitation.

'Then start your list with him.'

'But what if he won't come?'

'He will.' They all turned to the voice at the door. James Turner was leaning in the doorway, his arms folded across his chest. 'Just make the list, Dr Tyler, and leave the logistics to me.'

She glanced towards Luke, who gave her an almost imperceptible nod. James Turner looked like a quiet force to be reckoned with. Silent but deadly.

She gave a little nod. 'Give me half an hour, Mr Taylor. I need some peace and quiet to make sure I capture everything I need. You'll get your list.'

He moved sideways to allow her through the doorway and back out into the ER department. She stopped as she glanced around. 'My ER department is still open?' Her voice rose in hopefulness towards the end of the sentence.

'There haven't been any arrivals for the last hour, so there haven't been any problems. We're just about to move the First Lady. Once we've done that, there'll just be some extra security posted around the building. Your ER department can function as normal.'

'How about I hang out in the ER while you do that list, Abby?' Luke stood up from his chair and moved over next to her.

'Are you sure you don't mind?'

'No probs.' His hand brushed along her back as she headed out the door, sending more tingles down her skin that seemed to connect with her lips. This was ridiculous. She was a professional with work to do. Not some love-struck teenager. It was time she got back to the business in hand.

'And, children?' Both of them turned to David Fairgreaves's voice. 'You looked as if you'd been fighting when you came in earlier.' He folded his arms across his chest and smirked at them. 'It's time to kiss and make up, we've got work to do— work we need to do together, as a team.' And he put his head back down and began to write.

Luke sat at the main desk in the ER. Abby had been gone for nearly an hour and a half. The list was obviously taking longer than she thought. So far he'd stitched a finger, pulled a bead out of some kid's nose and dealt with some mild chest pain.

All of a sudden he had a whole new respect for the work Abby did. Children didn't co-operate like adults. They made a fuss, or had a tantrum, and generally didn't do a thing they were told. She had chosen this as her speciality?

He plastered a smile on his face as he heard a thump on the desk. Yes, there she was. The red-headed nurse that had been whispering and pointing at him for the last hour. The last thing that he needed right now.

'So you're Dr Storm?' She smiled as she twiddled a strand of her long red hair.

'That's right.' He wasn't going to do anything to encourage her.

'I'm Viv, one of the RNs.' She crossed her legs in front of him, clearly wanting to accentuate the long shapely limbs.

'Pleased to meet you, Viv.'

Thump. 'And I'm Carol.' A brunette slid along the desk next to Viv. Hadn't these staff ever heard of sitting on chairs? Great. Two for the price of one.

'So how do you know Dr Tyler?' asked Carol curiously.

'We were med students together in Washington.'

Carol's brow wrinkled. 'But Abby trained in San Francisco.'

He smiled. 'I know that. She started her training with me and transferred a little later.'

Viv moved in for the kill. 'So you won't know anyone else here, then?'

'No, no, I don't.'

'So where will you be staying tonight?'

The words were like a bolt out of the blue. Luke hadn't even given it a moment's thought. Where was he going to stay tonight? He glanced around, looking for James Turner—maybe he'd already made plans for his staff and included Luke in them?

'I'm not sure yet. But I think that something will already have been arranged.' *Please let something have been arranged.*

'If you don't have any plans for tonight, you could come to the hospital barbeque.'

'What?'

Luke was feeling momentarily distracted. Viv had just leaned forward and was revealing a certain amount of cleavage and he was feeling distinctly uncomfortable. It wasn't the first time a woman had been obvious around him. But here he was definitely out of his comfort zone. He couldn't walk away and talk to another colleague. He couldn't make an excuse and go and see to one of his many patients—he'd just checked on Dr Blair and he was sleeping. He didn't even have an office to go and retreat to. He was feeling like a fly caught in a spider's web. A red-haired spider's web.

'Will Abby be going to the barbeque?' It seemed like the safest option.

Viv and Carol exchanged glances and shrugged their shoulders. Carol stretched out her arms and glanced over his shoulder, clearly getting bored with uninteresting Luke. 'Abby doesn't usually go anywhere without Reuben,' she said, before turning on her heel and moving towards the reception doors as a car pulled up outside. 'Come on, Viv, let's see what's arrived.'

Viv shot a little smile at Luke before sliding off the desk and heading to the door.

But Luke had stopped paying attention. He was oblivious. Who was Reuben? He leaned his elbows on the desk and put his head in his hands. It had been one hell of a day. He glanced at his watch—

it wasn't even dinnertime yet. It had been eight a.m. when he'd got the call about Dr Blair. He had already been up since six, preparing to go and present a paper at a conference. A paper that was now lying in a crumpled heap in his bag. Seconds after he'd got the call one of the sleek black secret-service cars had pulled up, whisking him away to a helicopter pad bringing him to Pelican Cove and Abby…

Was she living with someone? Engaged? Married? Or maybe even just a boyfriend? After all, why would a girl who looked as good as Abby be single? He slapped himself on the forehead. She'd asked him if he was married when they'd been in the changing room together. After that kiss. But he hadn't asked her. He hadn't asked her anything. He'd just assumed.

A chill slipped down his spine. Abby had always wanted a family. It was the reason they were no longer together. She loved kids, she'd wanted to work with them and have a whole brood of them herself. A requirement that Luke couldn't meet. He hadn't even been able to bring himself to contemplate thoughts of a family. In the end he'd told

Abby he just wanted to focus on his career. And kids didn't fit into that.

He knew he'd broken her heart. She'd asked him to reconsider, told him that somehow they could have beautiful children together, and that had broken his heart even more. Because he didn't think he'd ever be ready for that. He'd already filled the role of a parent to his brother Ryan—and failed miserably. He just wasn't cut out for parenthood. Not after what had happened to Ryan. Not after the responsibilities he'd had to shoulder when Ryan had got sick and his parents had continued to spend their time on 'mercy missions' overseas or in other parts of the country. When the reality was, they should have been *there*, acting like parents to their two sons.

And, as much as Abby loved him, she wouldn't give up her dream of having a family. There had been no tears, no hysteria—that wasn't Abby's style. She'd just walked away, literally, into the sunset on top of that Washington hill. When he'd gone back to their apartment a few hours later, she was gone. And the empty drawers and wardrobe had haunted him for weeks.

Suppose Abby had her family now? And the

husband to match? Was that who Reuben was, her husband? Although her body seemed unchanged, she could still have a whole brood of children at home. The thought of Abby, with her husband and children, living in her white-picket-fenced house, made his blood run cold. He closed his eyes and tried to pull the memory from his dimly lit mind. Was there a ring on her finger? When they'd been in the changing room and she'd traced her finger along his scar, had there been a ring on that hand? Try as he might, he couldn't remember. And it was killing him.

'Dr Storm?'

Luke started to attention, pulling his head out of his hands. James Turner was standing over him in that slightly ominous way that he did so well.

'Oh, Mr Turner, I was just going to ask you about where we were going to stay tonight.'

It was the first time Luke had seen anything resembling an expression on the man's face. A slight quirk of the mouth. 'My men will stay here, Dr Storm. We are the First Lady's security detail. We have to be available around the clock. You… can stay anywhere you like.'

Great. James Turner hadn't included him in the

plans. He heard voices in the nearby corridor and turned to see Abby and Dr Fairgreaves obviously finalising a few things on the 'list'.

'Abby?'

She gave a final nod to David Fairgreaves and walked over towards them, holding out the list to James Turner. 'Everything and everybody I need. If you get them here, by the grace of God, we can deliver this baby safely.' She handed the list over and James Turner disappeared silently down the corridor, talking into his lapel pin and holding his earpiece. 'What's up, Luke?'

And there she was. Gone was the flustered, hot-under-the-collar woman from the changing room. Gone was the little sparks of jealousy he thought he'd seen in the canteen. This was his Abby. The woman he'd always known and admired. Calm, controlled Abby Tyler. He'd seen her stop at the scene of an accident and treat multiple victims, with no equipment whatsoever, speedily and com-petently. While he'd been stuck hanging onto the back end of car to stop it catapulting off the edge of a cliff. She'd disappeared from his side one day in the supermarket aisle and he'd found her moments later, resuscitating a man who'd had a cardiac arrest at the checkout. No panic, no stress, she'd just looked at him calmly and asked, 'Do you want to do the chest compressions or the mouth-to-mouth?'

What he'd never seen was how she'd been in the changing room.

She'd been angry with him. Or had it been frustration? It had been the first time they'd kissed in five years and he'd acted on instinct. From the first time he'd seen her that morning he'd felt as if someone had punched him square in the solar plexus. Abby Tyler with her feet up on the desk and her eyes closed, enjoying a moment of calm. He'd been stuck in his worst nightmare and she'd been the calmest woman on the planet.

Jennifer Taylor had been impressed. She'd called Luke into her room earlier to ask him what he knew about her. She was one smart lady and it was obvious she'd picked up on the undercurrents between them. She'd poked and prodded until Luke had finally confessed they'd once been an item.

'Silly boy,' she'd said as she'd lain back against her pillows with a smug look on her face.

'What do you mean?'

'She's gorgeous. And she's obviously a good

influence on you. You've stopped flapping, you're calm. She seems like a beautiful, intelligent woman and you've been a fool to let her slip through your fingers. What age are you? Twenty-nine? Thirty?'

He'd nodded. 'I'm thirty.'

'No one should live their life alone, Luke. I was the highest flyer of them all, but meeting Charlie was the best thing that ever happened to me. You need someone to share things with, the good and the bad, someone who's always in your corner no matter what. A career is a career, but a life? Now, that's worth living.'

Luke had been momentarily stunned by the frankness of her words. But then he'd asked himself why. Jennifer Taylor was known as a woman who pulled no punches. That's why she was so highly regarded. The story of how she and Charles Taylor had met had been widely reported in the past. She absorbed in her work; he in his politics. And when they'd met—*kaboom!* It had been a true partnership. She'd blossomed into a beautiful, fiercesome human-rights lawyer and he into a leader among men. So why was he surprised? And why was he feeling a little disappointed that Miss

Cool and Controlled was back? He'd liked the new version of Abby. He'd liked the new shouting, passionate, even jealous version of Abby. The added spark made her even more sexy than normal.

Something hit him on the side of his head. He bent to pick it up. The most sorry excuse of a paper airplane he'd ever seen. He smiled and looked up. Abby was leaning over the desk towards him.

'What are you so deep in thought about?'

'Why do you want to know?'

'Because I remember that look and it usually means trouble.' She walked around the side of the desk and sat down next to him. 'I think James Turner's going to get me everything on that list,' she whispered.

He bent towards her ear. 'I think he is too.' Her face was only inches from his.

'He's a little scary, isn't he?'

Luke nodded and smiled. He didn't want to move. If he leaned forward just the tiniest bit he could kiss her on the nose. His eyes flickered around him as he noticed a number of pairs of eyes on them. Somehow, when he was with Abby, it seemed as if it was just the two of them.

She reached over and touched his hand. 'Thanks

for looking after my patients while I did the list, Luke. It must have been a bit strange, being an ER doc.'

Luke looked at her hand as he felt the warmth travel upwards, causing the hairs on his arm to stand on end. *Relief, no ring.* He allowed himself to enjoy it as the warmth spread across his chest. 'Mmm, Abby, can I ask you something?'

'Sure.' She sat back in her chair, breaking the spell between them and making him feel as if somewhere a barrier had just came crashing down between them. His eyes hadn't left her and he watched as she tucked a loose tendril of hair behind her ear.

'Can you recommend a good guest house to me?'

'A guest house? What for?'

He rolled his eyes. 'It seems that James Turner didn't include me in the accomodation arrangements when organising where everyone would stay. So I need to find a guest house close by. Or do you have on-call rooms?'

She smiled sympathetically. 'We do, but unfortunately they've been commandeered by the Black Brigade.'

'Aah, so that's where they're staying.' He wrinkled his nose. 'How on earth are they all going to fit?'

'Apparently they're going to sleep in shifts.'

'Ugh.' he shuddered. 'I don't even want to think about that.'

'You can stay with me.' The words were out before she'd even had time to process the thought, or the practicalities. But it was just what Abby would always do—help out a friend in trouble. And that's what she was doing, wasn't she?

'What? No, Abby. I can't expect you to do that.'

But she'd stood up and was wiping her hands on her scrubs. 'Of course you can. We're old friends, aren't we? And you've been landed here in the middle of…unusual circumstances. The least I can do is help you out.'

'That's really nice of you, Abby. But won't it be a little awkward?'

This was it. This was when she told him she was married with ten kids. She hesitated, just for a tiny second, but he saw it and felt as if he'd been kicked in the guts.

'There's just one thing, Luke…'

'What's that?' *Let's hear it. Let's get it over with.*

'Mommy!' A human cannonball burst through one of the nearby doors, causing several of the security detail to jump out of their skins and slide their hands inside their jackets. It catapulted across the department in a flash of red and jumped straight into Abby's automatically outstretched arms.

'Reuben,' she said as he wrapped her in a bear hug and smothered her in kisses.

'Look, I've caught a crab!' he shouted, holding his bucket aloft.

Luke hadn't moved. He hadn't breathed. The human cannonball had white-blond hair and pale blue eyes.

CHAPTER FOUR

FOR Luke it was like a blast from the past. He felt as if he were looking at an old photograph of himself and his brother. Carbon copies of each other, with their white-blond hair and pale blue eyes. And now this. Reuben. Like a little mini-me. He was stunned as a million thoughts catapulted into his brain at once.

Abby was engrossed in her son and didn't seem to notice his reaction. When on earth had Abby had a child? And why didn't he know about it?

For a second, just for the tiniest second, a wild thought flitted through his brain. It was like looking into a mirror. He tried to approximate Reuben's age. Was he around four? Could, by some miracle, Reuben be his?

Almost as soon as the thought appeared, he shook it off. He was infertile. Tests had shown beyond any doubt that he was infertile. Reuben could never be his child. So whose child was he? And just how quickly had Abby moved on?

He cleared his throat, attracting her attention. 'You have a son.'

'Yes, yes, I do.' Abby turned Reuben around in her lap to face Luke with a proud smile on her face. 'Reuben, this is Mommy's friend. He's called Luke and he's a doctor, like Mommy.'

'Does he look after kids too?'

'No, he looks after hearts.'

'Wow.' Reuben eyed Luke suspiciously for a few seconds before he obviously decided he must be okay. 'Hi, Dr Luke.'

Luke watched the little figure Abby had clutched closely to her chest, his heart beating frantically. 'Pleased to meet you, Reuben.' He held his hand out to the little guy, who frowned at it before holding his own hand up for a high-five instead.

Luke slapped the hand held aloft and leaned closer. 'How old is Reuben, Abby?'

'He's four,' she answered quickly as she handed Reuben one of Nancy's home-made cookies.

Four. A new sensation flitted through him. She'd replaced him almost instantly.

Fury started to build inside him. All rational

thought was leaving the building. He was infertile. He couldn't have kids. That's the reason he'd broken up with her—because he couldn't fulfil her dreams of having a family. And he hadn't wanted to make her lose that chance.

And she obviously hadn't. Abby had moved on and had the family she deserved. So why did it hurt so much?

He felt a hand on his shoulder and looked up. James Turner—the Man in Black. 'We need to have a word.'

Luke nodded and scraped his chair along the floor as he stood, following James Turner to the nearby admin office.

'There's been a change of plan.'

'She's going to San Francisco?' Right now, Luke couldn't care less.

'If only. No, there's been a change of plan for you.'

'What do you mean?'

James Turner had the grace to avert his eyes. 'This has been a highly unusual situation.'

'You can say that again.'

He raised his hand to stop Luke speaking. 'Dr Storm, right now you are the only Presidential

doctor in the vicinity. We have a range of protocols for these circumstances. The most important
is that the First Family is looked after by doctors
that are obviously well qualified but who have also
been subject to our rigorous security checks.' He
looked along the corridor towards the cath lab.
'Dr Blair is physically unfit to serve as the First
Lady's doctor right now.'

Luke nodded in agreement.

'However, she is quite insistent that she values
his opinion and wishes him to be consulted regarding her condition.'

'That's well out with my realm of expertise, Mr
Turner. I'm happy to look after Dr Blair but I've
no idea about the First Lady. To be honest, we've
landed really lucky here. Dr Fairgreaves may be
retired but he's considered by many to be one of
the finest obstetricians in America, so you would
need to seek his opinion on the First Lady's condition.' Luke was in a hurry to get away. His mind
was on other things. The 'no ring' thing didn't
mean Abby wasn't married. He'd worked with lots
of female doctors who didn't routinely wear their
jewellery to work. Was he going to have to make
small talk with Abby's husband?

The unimpressed voice cut into his thoughts. 'I wouldn't call this luck, Dr Storm.'

'What?'

James Turner fixed him with a hard stare. 'This is not a situation that I would deem "lucky". In fact, I would deem this as anything but "lucky", Dr Storm.'

Luke scratched his chin. He had no idea what was going on here but, to be frank, he'd other things to worry about right now, like whether or not Abby was married. He couldn't possibly have any say in what happened with Jennifer Taylor. It was absurd. He knew nothing about obstetrics and only had a limited knowledge in paediatrics.

'Our protocols say you have to be on staff, Dr Storm. I hope you packed enough for four days— or maybe longer.'

Luke felt a cold sweat breaking out on his body. 'On staff? What does that mean? That's ridiculous! I'm happy to take care of Dr Blair for the next twenty-four hours—as a professional courtesy, of course—but anything else, forget it. I'm not your man.' He'd expected to have to stay overnight—but four days?

'Actually, Dr Storm, you are.' He waved a contract with a presidential seal at the bottom. 'It's in the small print. You can check with Captain Leon Gibbs if you want. He will clarify your position for you. No matter what your specialty, if you are the only presidential doctor available at the time, you have to stay on staff until a suitable replacement is found.'

'But you've got a suitable replacement in Dr Fairgreaves!' Luke's voice rose to crescendo pitch. Leon Gibbs was the navy captain who was the head of the White House medical unit—the man who had recruited him. The man was terrifying on a good day. He really didn't want to have to check anything with him.

'He hasn't had the necessary checks.'

'And how long does that take?'

The corner of James Turner's mouth lifted upwards. 'Longer than four days.'

'This is absurd!'

A flicker of exasperation passed over James Turner's face. 'Let me clarify exactly what I, and your country, expect from you, Dr Storm. You have to take care of Dr Blair. You have to make sure he is mentally competent to be consulted on Mrs Taylor's condition. Anything that could compromise his ability to consult—procedures, medications, et cetera—should be notified to me. You also have to be sure that all decisions taken are medically sound. If you have doubts, you can feel free to ask the opinions of others that you trust—as long as they sign a confidentiality agreement, that is.'

'So I've got to stay here for four days—or longer—until all this is over?' Luke ran his hand through his hair. A few hours ago he would have given anything to stay here for the next few days. But now? He didn't know what to think.

'That's right. You don't need to be *here*. You just need to always be available to me.' He handed Luke a new phone. 'Don't switch it off, Dr Storm, it has a tracker in it. Now I guess you'd better find somewhere suitable to stay.' He glanced over in Abby's direction. 'Somehow I don't think that will be too much of a problem, will it?'

Luke stalked back into the emergency department in time to see Abby kissing Reuben goodbye and waving out the window to him. He crossed to the window to see Reuben walking hand in hand along the coastal path with a young woman with long brown hair.

'Who's that?'

'What? Oh, that's Lucy. She's my childcare worker and she's awesome with Reuben. Childcare workers are like gold around here. I'm lucky to have her.'

Something twisted in Luke's gut. It was clear Abby was besotted with her son. Was she as besotted with his father?

'Where did you find her?'

Abby smiled. 'Being a paediatrician has its benefits. I looked after Lucy's brother a few years ago. She remembered me and offered her services when she heard I was looking for someone.' Abby turned to face Luke, touching his arm, 'Luke, I'm sorry I didn't tell you I had a child—I was just about to when he came barrelling through the doors.' She smiled. 'He's a real livewire.'

It was all Luke could do not to pull his arm from hers. Did she really have no idea how he was feeling? How could she be so blasé about this? He gritted his teeth. There was only one question he could ask. 'So are you going to introduce me to Luke's dad?'

'Luke's dad?' Abby looked astonished by the question. 'Well, that would be difficult since I don't know who he is.' She carried on looking over a patient's chart as if she'd just given the most natural answer in the world.

Luke felt as if he was going to explode. She didn't know who Reuben's father was? What the hell was going on? Had she just slept with some anonymous stranger? What had happened to the Abby Tyler he'd known?

It took Abby a few seconds to realise that something was wrong. She'd thought Luke had been a little off, but thought it was because she hadn't told him about Reuben. He'd baulked when she'd told him what age Reuben was, a reaction she hadn't understood at the time. And then the penny dropped. Hard.

No! He couldn't possibly think...

She put her head in her hands as she pictured her son in her mind. And then she cringed at the answer she'd just given about Luke's father. *What must he think of her? Did he think she'd slept with the first man that came along?*

Everyone here knew her, everyone knew her history and Reuben's background. But Luke had missed out on a whole chapter of her life. A whole five years.

'Luke.' She turned towards him with new eyes. This time she could see the rage that was bubbling under the surface, barely contained. She could see his brain trying to process everything around him—and coming to the wrong conclusion.

She placed her hand on his shoulder and saw him visibly flinch. 'I think I should explain. It's not what you think.'

'Reuben's four, Abby. You must have got pregnant as soon as you left.' He spat his words through clenched teeth.

Abby put both of her hands on his shoulders. 'Look at me, Luke.' Her voice was calm and steady. She stood square in front of him. 'Do you really think I'd do that?'

'It looks like it.'

She pressed down hard on his shoulders. 'Stop it. Stop it now. You know me. You know I would never do anything like that.'

'Well, how do you explain Reuben?'

Abby took a deep breath. 'You didn't want children, Luke, and I did. So I reassessed my life. I came here…' she pointed out the window at the ocean view '...to this beautiful place because I wanted to raise my children in the best place possible. I applied to adopt as soon as I had secured my position here and had a suitable house. It all takes time, Luke. I got Reuben when he was eighteen months old. I'm not his natural mother.'

'You adopted him?' his voice was incredulous. In the maelstrom of thoughts that had bombarded his mind he hadn't even considered the possibility.

She nodded slowly. 'It's best thing I ever did.' Her voice dropped. 'His age is just a coincidence.' She released her grip on his shoulders.

'Why on earth did you adopt?'

Abby sat down on one of the nearby chairs and crossed her legs. 'Why wouldn't I adopt?'

'Because you're young, you're beautiful. You could have come here and met someone else and had a baby of your own. I don't imagine for a minute that you've been short of offers.'

Abby flinched at his blunt words then nodded slowly, ignoring his last comment. 'Yes, yes, I could have. But I didn't. I didn't want to. This is what I wanted to do.'

'I don't understand.' Luke ran his fingers through his hair in frustration.

'There's lots of different ways to have a family, Luke.' Her voice was almost a whisper.

'But why this way? Why did *you* choose this way?'

Abby cast her eyes out the window. He was asking difficult questions, but then again he probably felt as if he was entitled to. And if she was going to answer honestly, it was easier not to look at him.

'I had a dream of having a happy family. But I wanted to have the happy husband to go with the happy family. And it didn't happen for me. And I realised that families come in all shapes and forms. I didn't need a husband for my family. Not all families are mom, dad and 2.4 kids. And not all kids are perfect. So I decided it was time to follow my heart.'

She was talking about him. She was talking about him and her. That had been her dream. And he'd ruined it for her. Ruined it by not taking the time to consider the options. Then the entirety of her words struck home. He'd been so focused on the first part of her sentence he hadn't paid attention to the second.

A chill went down Luke's spine. *Not all kids are*

perfect. 'What do you mean?' He walked across the room and knelt before Abby in her chair. 'What do you mean, "Not all kids are perfect"? Abby, what's wrong with Reuben?'

There was silence. The question hung in the air between them. Abby's eyes were fixed on the floor. He saw her swallow uncomfortably. 'He has ALL.' Her voice was barely audible.

This time Luke really did feel as if he'd been punched. That beautiful, bouncy little boy had ALL.

The room was spinning now. Acute lymphoblastic leukemia, the most common type of childhood cancer, the same type that had killed his teenage brother fifteen years ago.

Abby seemed to focus, to gain her perspective. She leaned forward, 'Luke, I'm sorry, I didn't want to tell you.'

Her brown eyes were filled with compassion and without a thought he did what seemed the most natural thing in the world and wrapped his arms around her.

'Oh, Abby, I'm so sorry.'

He could feel her tremble beneath his grip. She leaned her head on his shoulder and took a few deep breaths. He lifted his hand and stroked her blonde hair. They stayed that way for a few moments, Luke still kneeling on the floor with Abby wrapped in his embrace, then he put a hand on either side of her head and lifted it from his shoulder, placing a gentle kiss on her forehead.

'So how is he doing?'

Her eyes were bright with unshed tears. She sat back in her chair but kept hold of Luke's hand. 'He's doing well. He's been getting treatment for the last two years. You can see he's a lively little boy.' She gave nervous laugh. 'It's difficult to keep an eye on him. What I really want to do is wrap him up in cotton wool and hide him somewhere, keep him safe from infections and injuries, but that's just not Reuben. He's a livewire and I've got to let him live his life.'

He clasped her hand even tighter. He could see the conflicting emotions in her face. The parent and the doctor. 'Did you know he was sick when you adopted him?'

Abby shook her head. 'He wasn't initially, but you know how long these things can take. He'd had a medical before the adoption procedures began and everything was fine. He'd already been staying with me for a few months when I started to notice all the classic signs—the bruising, frequent infections and fever—and I just knew.' Her eyes glassed over. 'They asked me if I wanted to withdraw, can you imagine?' She turned to face him. 'As if I would do that. Then I guess they thought about it and decided who better to have a sick child than a paediatrician?'

Her voice wobbled. 'He was mine, Luke. From the first time I set eyes on him he was mine.' She broke her gaze from his, embarrassed by her reactions. Luke was the person who didn't want children, so he couldn't possibly understand how she felt.

'I didn't want to tell you about Reuben. I didn't want to bring back bad memories for you about Ryan.'

Ryan. She'd said it. The name cut straight through to his heart like a knife, a knife that plunged in to the hilt and was then twisted around. His brother. The little brother he'd played with, laughed with and shared everything with. They'd been inseparable, probably due to the fact that their parents had seemed to have so little time for them. The life of a senator and his wife was never quiet. So they'd depended on each other entirely. And Luke had let him down.

He squeezed her hand. 'Most memories of Ryan are good,' he said quietly.

She smoothed her ruffled hair back into place and put on a bright smile. It was obvious she was trying to clear her head. 'Did you bring an overnight bag with you?'

'What?' Luke started, still lost in thoughts of his brother and the life that had been stolen from him.

'A bag, Luke. Did you bring a bag with you?'

He nodded. 'I was due to speak at a conference and had my bag packed for that. It must still be stuck in the back of one of the secret-service cars.'

'Well, why don't you go and find it? You'll need it for tonight if you're staying at my place.' She turned and headed towards the door. 'And, Luke…' she gave him a little smile '…go and grab some scrubs, will you? I don't want you parading about my house in your usual nightwear—I've got a four-year-old, remember?' And with that parting shot she disappeared out the door, leaving Luke to stare out over the waves breaking in Pelican Cove.

He stood for a few minutes, watching the sea.

The irony of all this was that Ryan would have loved living in a place like this. And if he'd got sick a few years further down the line, there would have been more effective treatments, with better options and outcomes for the patients. Ryan could maybe have fulfilled his dream to be a surfer. He'd been the cleverest in the family by a mile. Naturally clever. One of these kids that had hardly needed to study and just sucked in information from all around them. But what he'd really wanted was to be a jock.

He'd wanted to play every sport known to man. And he'd done that for a while. But once he'd become sick, sports had been a no-no. Anything that could have caused injury, breaks, anything that had expended too much energy. All had been forbidden. So Ryan had only been able to dream about the sports he'd yet had to master. And surfing had been one of them.

Only once had the brothers had the opportunity to try surfing together. They'd been dragged to yet another official engagement by their parents—only this time it had been in Hawaii and the boys had disappeared to the beach as soon as they'd got there.

He'd never forget the look on Ryan's face as he'd finally managed to stand upright on the surfboard. The expression of pure joy and exhilaration, captured in a few fleeting seconds on his teenage brother's face, was a picture that was seared into Luke's brain. A moment in time, frozen and remembered for ever.

Luke tore his eyes away from the crashing waves. Sometimes the memories were just too hard.

Abby headed back down the corridor, her heart beating furiously in her chest. She wasn't sure if it was the effect of Luke holding her again, or from the stress of having to tell him about Reuben.

She ducked around the corner and stood for a second with her back against the wall, letting the feel of the cool concrete spread between her shoulder blades and back, easing her hot, trembling skin. She took a few deep slow breaths to calm her frantic heartbeat. At least he understood. At least he knew what it felt like to have someone that you love suffer from the condition. She didn't need to explain to him what type of cancer it was, the statistics around it, the treatments and, worst of all, what Reuben's chances were, because he knew all that already. Fifteen years ago the statistics had been much grimmer—Luke's brother was proof of that. Things were a lot more positive now, but there was still always the chance that her child would be the unlucky one. Abby shook the thoughts from her head. She couldn't stand it when the crows of doubt crept into her head and haunted her. A few months ago she'd had a dream that she was standing next to a graveside, watching a little white coffin being lowered into it, and she'd woken screaming and covered in sweat.

Why? She had no idea, because Reuben was doing well, brilliantly, in fact. But there was always just this tiny sliver of doubt, right at the back of her mind, chipping away at her. The slightest temperature and she'd be awake all night, worrying it was some hideous infection rather than a mild sniffle. But then again she was a mother and she was only human.

James Turner rounded the corner and just about walked into her. 'Dr Tyler, I was looking for you.' He seemed oblivious to her anxiety.

'You were? Is everything all right?'

'I'm just about to move Jennifer Taylor from

your emergency department, but she'd like to speak to you before she moves.'

'The First Lady, the First Lady wants to see me? But why? I'm not her doctor.'

'I know that, Dr Tyler.' He shrugged his shoulders. 'What the First Lady wants, the First Lady gets.'

Abby nodded and glanced at her watch. Nearly three o'clock. Only a few more hours before she could clock off and head home to Reuben, only this time she would have Luke in tow. She couldn't even begin to imagine what that would feel like. What would it be like to have a man under her roof? A man who was going to stay the night, and possibly for the next four days?

'Dr Tyler?' James Turner's voice was abrupt, he was obviously losing his patience.

'Sure, sure, I'm coming.'

Abby strode back into the emergency department and towards Jennifer Taylor's room. The security service man at the door gave her a little nod as he stood aside to let her enter the room.

Jennifer was on the phone and she was in tears. 'Yes, yes, I know. I understand, really I do.' She sniffed back a new wave of tears as Abby grabbed some tissues and crossed to the edge of the bed. 'Yes, Charlie, I promise, I'll get them to phone you if I go into labour. Love you.'

She hung up the phone and grabbed the tissues from Abby, blowing her nose furiously. 'I'm sorry Abby,' she motioned for her to sit down at the side of the bed.

'What are you sorry for? Was that your husband?'

She nodded tearfully.

'Is he mad at you?'

Jennifer shook her head. 'Charlie? Never. No, he's in the middle of a peace agreement, they've been negotiating it for the last two years and it's just about to be signed. So he really needs to be there. But he wants to be with me.'

Abby nodded. 'I'll bet he does. I'm surprised he doesn't want you near him in Washington.'

Jennifer laughed. 'That's the last place he wants me right now. No, he's spoken to Dr Fairgreaves and knows that I will get the best possible care. It's actually lucky that I'm here.'

'Lucky?'

'Yes. If this had happened in Washington, some

idiot would have leaked it to the press already. At least here I've got a modicum of privacy.'

Abby smiled. It was really the last thing she'd expected her to say. 'So you're happy that the First Son or Daughter is going to be born in Pelican Cove?'

'I couldn't be happier.'

Abby mulled it over. Jennifer Taylor was full of surprises. 'So what can I do for you?'

Jennifer rolled her eyes. 'I'm bored, Abby. They...' she motioned towards the door '...are driving me crazy. They won't let me out of the room, they won't let me open the window, they won't let me *look out* the window.' She flopped her head back against her pillows. 'There's a good chance I'm going to be here for at least four days. I can't take much more of this seclusion. I need something—or someone—to distract me.'

Abby smiled and looked around the little room. It was cheery enough, but was built for practicalities, not for comfort. She also knew that the room Jennifer Taylor was being moved to was almost identical.

'How about I bring you some movies from home, and some books? What do you like?'

Jennifer breathed an audible sigh of relief. 'Perfect, Abby, thanks. Movies, I like older ones, from when I was a teenager, particularly action ones—Bruce Willis, Harrison Ford or anything sci-fi. And books, definitely romance. You've got some, haven't you?'

'Oh, yes, by the bucketload.'

'You're a lifesaver. Thanks, Abby. I know there are things I should be worrying about. But I want some normality, some distractions. So, now I've got the *somethings* to distract me, what about the *someone*?'

'What do you mean?'

'Well, what's the gossip in Pelican Cove? Tell me. Tell me about the people and their lives. It's so nice just to talk to someone normal—about normal things.' She waved her arms around. 'Everybody that's usually around me has a political agenda. Either that, or they're trying to write *me* a political agenda. I want normal. I want to know girlie stuff. I'm away from Washington now. I'm in a beautiful part of the country I've never seen before. I don't want to be the First Lady right now. I want to be an expectant mom, waiting for her first child.'

She leaned over and touched Abby's hand. 'So, Dr Tyler, what's the story with you and our Dr Storm?'

Abby stiffened, taken aback by the question. 'Well, nothing really. We were friends a long time ago,' she stumbled.

'That's not what he says. He says you were *more* than friends.'

'He said what?' She was horrified. Luke had been discussing their past relationship with the First Lady?

'Don't look so worried. I'd noticed something between you and I asked him about it. He looked really down.'

'He did?' Maybe she wasn't so angry with him after all.

'I told him he was a fool to let you slip through his fingers.'

Abby half smiled. 'You did?' How could a woman that was only a few years older than her seem so worldly wise?

'Yes, I did.' Jennifer leaned over and grabbed a barrette from the nearby table, coiling her hair up at the back of her head and pinning it in place. 'He strikes me as quite a lonely soul,' she said, looking thoughtful. 'And knowing who his parents are, it doesn't come as such a surprise.'

Abby was startled. 'You know Luke's parents?'

'Of course I do. His father's a senator. Didn't you know that?'

Abby nodded her head. 'Yes, yes, I did. I met them at birthdays, Thanksgiving and Christmas. I was with Luke for four years but his parents weren't the most engaging people I've ever met. Kind of ironic since they're both politicians. When they spoke to me it was almost as if their minds were on something else—the next thing on their list. Let's just say that Luke didn't seem to have a very good relationship with them. We certainly didn't get invited around every week for Sunday dinner.'

'I'm not surprised. Senator Storm is charm himself, but it's all superficial. And as for her...' She gave her head a little shake then gave Abby's arm a little squeeze. 'Meeting you was probably the best thing that could have happened to him, Abby, and it's time to get to the bottom of whatever he's hiding from you.'

Abby looked incredulous. 'What on earth makes you think...?'

Jennifer Taylor tapped the side of her nose. 'I'm not the First Lady for nothing.'

Abby stood up and gave her a smile and she headed to the door, 'No, you're certainly not.'

The rest of the afternoon passed in a blur. Luke went between the ER and the cath lab, checking on Dr Blair. Abby spent most of her afternoon treating a nine-year-old who'd been stung by a jellyfish. She'd done the best she could following the latest protocols for carefully removing the tentacles, helping to prevent more venom release and treating the child with painkillers and steroids before arranging the transfer to San Francisco Children's Hospital for further treatment. And at the end of the day it didn't matter what she did, she already knew that the scarring would be significant.

Luke came and stood outside with her while she watched the ambulance pull away and draped his arm around her shoulders again.

'Are you okay?'

She gave a wistful little nod. 'I guess.' She watched the ambulance set off down the coastal road, 'I just wish that I could help more.'

He gave her shoulder a little squeeze. 'C'mon, Abby, you do the best job that you can. How can that be bad?'

She turned and shot Luke a smile that made his heart stop. He could almost feel the static in the air between them. If he just bent forward he could kiss her, right here, right now, in the middle of the ambulance bay outside the ER. Would she let him? Or would she object?

Her hair caught in the wind and fluttered in front of her face, blocking his direct access to her pink lips. She gave her head a shake and moved the strands from in front of her eyes, tucking them behind her ears. Their gaze was broken, the moment lost.

Something twisted in his stomach. Five years ago he would have been able to kiss Abby whenever he wanted. Now he couldn't. He'd no right to kiss her. He'd no right to hold her the way he was doing. He glanced at his arm resting easily on her shoulders, almost as if it was something he did every day. And there it was again—the feeling that he was missing something. That he'd let something really important just slip through his fingers. For someone on the outside, Jennifer Taylor wasn't too slow.

He turned slightly, guiding Abby back in towards the doors, and glanced at his watch. It was nearly six o'clock. 'Have we finished for the day?' he asked.

Abby nodded, glancing down at her pager. 'They'll call me if any paediatric emergencies come in that they can't cope with.' She turned to face him as they reached the desk. 'How's Dr Blair?'

'Textbook, no problems. Routine care, but the staff will call me if they have any concerns.'

'Have you got your case?'

Luke gave a little nod and pulled it from behind one of the desks. He shook his head slowly. 'Before you see the contents, all I can say in my defence is that I packed it for a conference, *not* for coming to Pelican Cove. I might be a little overdressed.'

'I can't wait to see. Come on, let's go.' She grabbed her jacket and headed towards the nearest exit. Luke expected her to head towards the car park but instead she headed for the coastal footpath that Reuben and his childcare worker had walked along earlier.

'What, no car?'

Abby smiled. 'I have one at home but here I don't need one. We're only about two minutes along this path.' She walked ahead along the path, which, although it lay well back from the cliffs, gave a spectacular view over the whole of Pelican Cove. From here Luke could see the boats sitting in the harbour, the houses dotted along the coast, the sandy beaches and even the pelicans on the rocks beneath.

'Wow, Abby, this is some view. You must love walking to and from work every day. You don't get this in Washington or San Francisco.'

'No, you don't.' She stopped and gazed towards the ocean. 'That's why I love it here—why I intentionally came to stay here when I knew I wanted to adopt.' She spread her arms out across the harbor. 'This is the kind of life I want for my kids,' she said. 'Not granite, stone, skyscrapers and streets that aren't safe to play in.'

'Kids? Plural? Are you planning on adopting some more or having some of your own?' It was a weighted question.

Abby shrugged her shoulders. 'Whatever happens happens. If it's only Reuben and me for as long as I'm blessed with him, then that's fine. If I meet someone and have some kids of my own, then that's fine too. If I don't ever meet someone, then I might decide to go down the route of adoption again. It's worked out pretty great for me this time.' She'd moved down the path a little and then stopped just short of a white picket fence. The fence surrounded a gorgeous shingled house that looked out over the ocean. It was painted blue and white and was large and spacious, much bigger than Luke would ever have expected, and looked like a true family home.

He could see Reuben playing in the garden with his childcare worker, jumping from a wooden-built swing to a little playhouse built in exactly the style of the main house, complete with little tiles on the roof.

Abby noticed him watching her blond, bouncing son. 'Like I said earlier, Luke, families come in all shapes and sizes and I'm happy to take what I'm given.'

The words stuck in his throat. This was where he should take the opportunity to talk, to tell her what a failure he'd been when the mumps had struck, and why he shouldn't be part of anyone's family—that when his brother had needed him most he had failed him.

It had killed him that he'd been so infectious he hadn't been allowed to visit his brother. The irony of it was he had been immunised against mumps as a child, but the vaccine obviously hadn't been effective. So, when he had been struck down with the highly infectious acute disease, the last person he had been allowed to visit had been his immunocompromised brother.

And with the mumps virus had come fever, swelling of his salivary glands and more importantly orchitis, inflammation of the testes. And Luke had been unlucky, in more ways than one. His sperm-producing cells had been damaged, leading to permanent infertility. At the time, it had all seemed so irrelevant. He'd just lost his brother. He hadn't really been interested in his family-making capabilities. But as time had progressed and he'd met Abby, a woman who wanted to have a family of her own, he'd known he couldn't take that away from her.

And he still wasn't ready to face up to his infertility. He'd followed the doctor's instructions for a year after the virus struck. Suffering the embarrassment of delivering samples of semen to check if his fertility status improved. Then the offer of counselling, when it hadn't. At that point, the last thing he'd wanted to discuss had been his lack of baby-making facilities. For him, it was linked. He'd failed in the parenting role for his brother and someone was making sure he wouldn't be in that position again.

He looked out over the cove again, watching the early-evening surfers catching the waves. This was where Ryan should have been. Leading the charge on the crest of a wave and riding his way to happiness and fulfilment.

Luke gave a little smile as he watched them, the strong sea winds raking through his hair. His eyes caught a glimpse of Abby's neat butt as she turned up a path away from the sea. He could almost hear his brother shouting in his ear: *Go for it, Luke!* Another smile spread across his face as he turned and followed her up the winding path.

CHAPTER FIVE

IT WAS just how he'd imagined it would be. A beautiful, light, airy house with gorgeous views over the ocean. Complete with white picket fence surrounding the garden. And the family to complete it.

It disturbed him a little. She was living in the house he'd always imagined her having. And everything about it was perfect, from the beautiful wooden floors and wide open spaces to the bright, carefully planted flowerbeds and sandpit in the front garden. Abby led him through the wide hallway to the kitchen at the back of the house. It was huge, with thick wooden worktops, a white Boston sink and a couple of easy chairs looking out of the patio doors over the back garden.

'Abby, just how big is this house?'

She gave a little smile. 'Big enough.'

'No, seriously, Abby, my apartment in Washington could fit in here six times over.'

She leaned back against her sink, crossing her arms over her chest. 'Well, there's this, the kitchen/diner, then I have two separate sitting rooms at the front and a study, a cloakroom and a laundry room. Upstairs there are five bedrooms, two en suites and a family bathroom.'

'Wow. This place is huge.' He cleared his throat a little. 'Without being cheeky, did you win the lottery?'

She laughed. 'I wish. Why would you think that?'

'Because this house is pretty near "Millionaires' Row" in Mendocino Valley. This place couldn't have come cheap.'

Abby walked over to the nearby stove and lifted the lid on a pot, inhaling deeply and giving it a stir. 'Actually, it came really cheap. I inherited it, it was my aunt's.'

His brow furrowed. 'Your aunt? I don't remember you talking about an aunt.'

'She was really my mom's best friend. This was her house. She never married and she never had any children. She was a writer. Do you remember those children's books with the big spider on the front?'

Luke gave a little nod. 'I remember you had a set of those on the bookshelves in our apartment.'

Abby walked over to a small bookcase next to one of the easy chairs looking out over the back garden. She pulled out a set of books with a big pink spider on the front. 'She wrote these nearly forty years ago and it made her a fortune. That's how she could afford this house. When she died she left it to me.'

Luke walked over next to her and looked out over the equally perfect back garden. 'God, I would kill for a place like this, Abby. It's gorgeous.'

Abby nodded, then turned back to the stove and gave the contents of the pot another stir. 'You're right, it is gorgeous. The perfect place to bring up a family.'

The words hung in the air between them. A thousand things unsaid. A thousand questions unanswered and misunderstood.

The hairs on her arms stood on end. Would he speak? Would he say anything about the past? About why he would never consider the other options to have children?

No, nothing. Luke said nothing, His eyes drifted

from the garden to the kitchen stove and then to his feet.

She tapped him on the shoulder. 'Come on upstairs and I'll show you to your room.' She bent to pick up his case.

Luke moved quickly. 'Don't be silly, I'll carry that.' His hand encircled hers and their eyes locked for a second. His pale blue eyes with her warm brown ones. Abby flinched, not really understanding why. She pulled her hand back.

'Come this way.' She led him up the white-painted stairs and into a corridor with white walls and a pale blue carpet. His eyes were drawn immediately to the beautiful round stained-glass window at the end of the corridor. The sun was streaming through the window, sending a cavalcade of rainbow hues pooling on the white walls.

'You've got a stained-glass window?' A few quick strides took him to the end of the corridor to touch the coloured glass. He peered at the image in the window. 'Flowers? What are these?'

Abby touched them in turn. 'The yellow ones are daffodils and the blue ones are bluebells. My aunt was born in Scotland and she used to live next to some fields that were full of these flowers. She got the window made to remind her of home.'

He looked down the corridor. The window at the other end was the same round shape and size, but only plain glass.

'How come she didn't do that one?'

Abby smiled. 'She meant to—she just didn't get around to it. I've always meant to do it myself. I'd love to have a field of colourful freesias—lots of reds, pinks and purples. But stained glass is just so expensive, and I've been distracted by other things.'

Luke nodded slowly. Having a sick child could steal every minute of your day. 'That's some piece of history.' He glanced around at some of the open doors. 'Which one is mine?'

Abby walked over to the furthest away door. 'In here.'

The room had pale blue walls, a wooden floor and white bedspread. Beautiful and homely, if a little impersonal. She walked over to the window. 'I thought you might like the room with the view.'

And there it was, the beautiful ocean view that only a house sitting on the hills could capture.

Abby smiled as she saw Luke take a deep breath. She pointed downwards. 'There's even a window seat.'

He gave a little nod. 'The view's gorgeous, Abby.' He watched the waves breaking in the ocean beneath them. People paid a fortune for a view like this. Abby had certainly landed on her feet.

'You've got to let me thank you for this.'

'What do you mean?'

'For letting me stay here.'

She gave a playful smile. 'It might only be for the one night, Luke. I throw guests out for bad behaviour, you know.'

He reached over and took her hand. 'I know that there's a hospital barbeque tonight. Do you want to go to that?'

She shook her head. 'No. I try not to socialise too much at those kinds of things. They tend to be more for the adults.' Her eyes glanced down-wards to the garden where Reuben was playing and he immediately understood. She wanted to spend some time with her son.

'How about if you let me take you somewhere local for dinner, then?' He lifted his hand as she went to interrupt. 'We could go out later, once you've put Reuben to bed, and you could ask Lucy to come back for a few hours. How about that?'

Abby nodded slowly. A late dinner would be fine. It would give her a chance to bath Reuben and put him to bed. Actually, a late dinner would be kind of nice. She couldn't remember the last time she had gone to dinner with someone.

The front door opened and slammed again as Reuben came running inside.

'Where are you, Mommy?' His little voice drifted upstairs.

'I'm here, honey.' She crossed into the corridor and leaned over the balustrade. 'I was just showing Dr Luke his room.'

'Dr Luke is staying tonight? Whoopee! Can he play cars?'

Luke shifted uncomfortably. Kids weren't his specialty and he didn't routinely spend time in their company. What if Reuben hated him?

He turned as Abby gave him a weak smile. 'Welcome to the madhouse.'

Luke pushed open the door to the restaurant and was immediately hit by the aromas of Mexican food. His stomach growled loudly and Abby laughed.

'That's twice in one day. Are you hungry, Luke?'

'Starving. I take it you know this place well?'

She gave a little smile. 'Of course I do. We eat here nearly every week.' She walked to the back of the restaurant and shouted through the doors to the kitchen, 'Diego, sorry we're late. Reuben wouldn't go to bed.'

Luke could hear some muffled response and Abby led him to a red and white chequered table near the front of the restaurant. There were several other couples in the eatery, all at various stages of dinner, many huddled over flickering red candles on the tabletops, several of whom raised their hands, waving at Abby.

Luke felt something strange in his stomach. Uneasiness. Abby had a whole range of friends and acquaintances that he knew nothing about. She'd built a life for herself and for Reuben in this friendly little community. Five years ago they'd moved in the same circles and had had the same group of friends. Now everything had changed and he knew nothing about the life that she led.

A tall Mexican man appeared at their table, carrying a pitcher of water and two glasses. 'It's nice to see you again.' He bent over and kissed Abby on the cheek. 'Here you go, Abby.' He placed the glasses and pitcher on the table and winked at Luke. 'In preparation for the extra-hot food she likes.'

Abby gave a wide smile. 'Can I have a diet soda too, please, Diego?' She glanced over at Luke. 'What would you like?'

'Diet soda's fine for me too, thanks.' His eyes swept around the restaurant, noticing there were no menus or wine lists on the table. And almost instantly he understood. This wasn't the type of establishment where you ordered. You only told them whether you liked your food medium, hot or very hot. His head tilted towards Diego. 'So what's on the menu tonight, then?'

'Aha, that will be a surprise for the lovely couple.' He pointed at them both. 'Do you have any allergies the kitchen should know about, sir?'

Luke shook his head.

'And how spicy do you like your food?'

His eyes swept over the pitcher of iced water already on the table. Last time he'd gone for dinner with Abby she wouldn't even order a curry.

'I'll have what she's having,' he said with confidence.

She flung back her head and laughed. 'I warn you, Luke, my tastes have changed in the last few years. I doubt you'll be able to keep up.'

'Is that a challenge?'

She leaned back in her chair. 'It could be.' She reached over and touched Diego's hand. 'I'll leave this all in your capable hands.'

He gave a little nod and headed off towards the kitchen.

Abby lifted the pitcher and poured some iced water into the two glasses. 'So what have you been doing in Washington, Luke?'

He raised his eyebrow. 'I think we better start with what you've been doing for the last five years, Abby.'

She shifted under his steady gaze. This was about Reuben again. Why was he so astonished that she'd adopted a child? She'd never made any secret of the fact she wanted to have children.

'I would have thought that was obvious, Luke. I found the job of my dreams, inherited the house of my dreams and was able to realise my own personal dream and adopt a child.' She took a sip from her glass of water. 'I think you could say I've been pretty busy.'

He watched as she brushed her blonde hair back from her face. She'd changed into a light summer dress and cardigan before they'd walked down to the restaurant. And he could smell the strawberry lip gloss again. But his eyes had caught sight of something else. A thin gold chain around her neck, holding a gold locket that dipped into her cleavage. Before he could stop himself, he reached over, lifted the delicate chain and caught the locket between his lean fingers. 'You still wear this?'

Her cheeks flushed gently with colour.

'I thought you would have thrown it away years ago.'

Her fingers touched his, lifting the locket from him. He'd bought it for her years earlier and it used to hold a picture of them together inside.

'Why would I get rid of it? I always loved this locket.' Her fingernails caught the edge and split it open. 'I've just got a different picture inside it now.'

She turned the locket towards him. A picture of a mischievous little boy with blond hair and a red T-shirt grinned back at him.

The words caught in Luke's throat. Again, it was as if he was gazing at a picture from his past. He cleared his throat. 'Reuben. That's a lovely picture.'

Her eyes fell downwards. 'Yes, it is, isn't it?' She gave him a sad smile. 'It seemed most appropriate. After all, lockets are supposed to hold the picture of the ones most dear to your heart. Aren't they?'

Their picture had been replaced by a child's. Did that mean she didn't have room in her heart for anyone else?

The silence was broken as Diego reappeared and placed some steaming bowls on the table along with a basket of rolls. 'Here we go, folks, pumpkin and chorizo soup.'

Luke leaned over the bowl and breathed deeply. 'That smells fantastic, Diego, and not at all what I expected.'

Abby gave Diego a little nod. 'Many thanks, Diego.' She reached for one of the bolillo rolls served with the soup. 'I've learned to expect the unexpected coming here. There's always some-thing just a little quirky.' She blew on the spoon-ful of soup she'd just lifted from the bowl, before taking a sip. 'Wow, you can taste the garlic, cumin and oregano. This is gorgeous.'

Luke reached over and broke open one of the crusty bolillo rolls, dipping it into his soup. 'So are you going to tell me any more about how you got here?'

Abby shook her head. She didn't feel like getting into all that. Especially not in the middle of a restaurant. Her hand went automatically to the locket around her neck. Luke had no idea that his picture was still in there, underneath the picture of Reuben. Still close to her heart.

'I think it's time we talk about you, Luke.'

He put his spoon down. 'What do you want to talk about?'

'I want to know how you've been these last five years. Why you felt you couldn't keep in touch. Why you ignored every email and message I left you.'

Luke could feel the hairs on his arms stand on end at her questions. She hadn't raised her voice or caused a scene. She'd just asked the questions in her normal, matter-of-fact manner. But how could he tell her that she'd broken his heart when she'd walked away? He'd pretended that it was all about the fact she'd wanted children and he hadn't. And he'd kept his defences high, because it had been the only way to get through it.

'I told you earlier I thought it was best if we had a clean break, Abby. There was no point in sending constant emails or talking on the phone. We both agreed that we wanted different things.'

'Wanting different things didn't mean we couldn't be friends.'

'It was too hard. I needed to focus on my career.' Then he hesitated. 'It's like I tried to say earlier, if we'd kept in touch it would have been difficult for either of us to move on. I know you were just trying to be friendly, but to go from what we had... to being friends—it was just a step too far for me. I needed a clean break. I thought it would be best for you too. I thought you would meet someone else and have the family you always wanted.' He met her eyes in the flickering candlelight. 'It broke my heart when you walked away.'

Silence. So quiet you could have heard a pin drop.

Abby put down her spoon and reached out and touched his hand. 'I didn't leave because you couldn't have children, Luke. I left because you wouldn't even have that discussion with me. You wouldn't even consider the possibilities.' Her fingers traced a line up from his wrist to his palm. It felt like, right now, she had to be touching him. She really wanted to plant herself in his lap and wrap her arms around his shoulders—but there was a table in the way. 'You broke my heart too, you know?'

'I know,' he whispered. 'I just didn't expect this.'

'Expect what?'

He pulled his hand back and sat back in his chair. 'You, to have a family—like this. I thought you would have met someone, got married and been pregnant.'

Abby felt the hairs stand up on the back of her neck. She could say a hundred things here. Tears glistened in her eyes. But there was only one thing she wanted to say. It didn't matter how inappropriate it was. It didn't matter that Luke was only here for a few days. He was here, right now, for the first time in five years.

She sucked in a deep breath. 'How could I do that, Luke? How could I meet someone else and fall in love? My heart was always going to belong to you.'

'Wow.' She saw his shoulders tense.

'Wow? That's all you can say—wow?'

A sexy smile spread across his face. He stood up, leaned across the table and planted a kiss straight on her surprised lips.

'Sometimes actions speak louder than words, Abby.' He sat back down in his chair.

The way he staring at her was unnerving her. She didn't feel as if she was sitting in a restaurant. She felt as if they were the only two people in the room.

Abby went to speak but Diego appeared from out of nowhere to remove the plates from their table. 'You enjoy, yes?'

Abby nodded in response, trying to break the heavy silence. 'What's next?' she asked.

'Our specialty, fajitas.'

'My favourite. Fab, thanks, Diego.' She watched as he sauntered back to the kitchen. She gulped. Time to change the subject. 'How's your relationship with your parents these days?'

The warmth between them vanished in an instant. His icy blue eyes met hers. 'How do you think it is?'

She shrugged. Absolutely the wrong thing to

say. It was obvious there was no improvement, but she'd never found out why and after all this time it felt as if it was time to dig a little deeper.

'I think I don't know, Luke, because you've never talked about it. But we're five years older and five years wiser.' She reached across the table and caught his hand in hers. 'So do you want to tell me what's so bad about them?'

'You've met them, you should understand.'

Her brow furrowed. 'Yes, I've met them and thought they were a little cold. But I never really got to know them.'

'Lucky you,' he mumbled.

She squeezed his hand a little harder. 'That seems a strange thing to say about your parents.'

Luke threw his hands up. 'Well, they're not exactly regular parents, are they? Ryan and I hardly saw them when we were kids. The life of a senator is very busy. I knew my nanny better than I knew my parents.'

'That's horrible.'

She could feel the tension in the air. There was an inevitable question that followed that statement. 'How were they when Ryan was sick?'

'Busy. They were always busy.' The words were almost spat out.

Abby swallowed hard. 'Too busy to look after their child when he was sick?' The words were alien to her, almost filled with disbelief. She'd been in the situation herself and couldn't imagine a parent not wanting to be at their child's sickbed.

The look of disgust on Luke's face was evident. 'They were hardly ever there. Do you know the first time Ryan needed a bone-marrow aspiration my mother ran from the room and left me there with Ryan? I've never forgiven her for that. They went to a few hospital appointments, spoke to a few doctors and then carried on with business as usual. I was more of a parent to Ryan than they were. I went with Ryan for all his treatments— well, most of them.' The words were left hanging in the air.

Luke hadn't moved. He was still lost in his thoughts. Her fingertips brushed over the top of his clenched fist that lay on the table. He blinked at the feather-like touch, automatically releasing his hand.

'You said most of them?'

'What?' Her touch had jerked him back out of

that black place. The one where he was a teenager, laden with responsibility and guilt. Trying
to fill the space left by two absent adults. Her dark
brown eyes were pulling him in, pulling him into
a place he didn't want to go to.

She was doing it again. Looking at him as though
she could see right into the heart of the matter,
right into his soul. Her fingers were now concen-
trating on his outstretched index finger, running
gently up and down it in a soothing manner.

'You said most of the time. I kind of get the im-
pression you've not said everything you need to.
Were you with Ryan when he died?'

His fingers clenched again, hiding themselves
inside his fist. Abby wanted to pull the words back
into her mouth. A dark and heavy cloud loomed
over them. She knew the answer to that question
without him even having to formulate a sentence.

'I wasn't allowed to be with Ryan. It was about
the only time my parents did finally come home.'

Her mind tried to make sense of what he'd just
said. 'What do you mean, *you weren't allowed*?'

She could see his heavy eyelids. She knew that
behind them there were tears forming. *Please
don't let me see him cry.*

'That's when I had mumps. I couldn't be near Ryan when he was immunocompromised. So I had to phone my mom and dad and ask them to come home.' He ran his fingers through his hair. 'They were their usual busy selves. I don't think any of us realised just how sick Ryan actually was.'

Abby stretched her arms across the table and took both his hands again. He could see the pain in her eyes, the empathy from a mother who could find herself in that position too.

'I hope you're both hungry.' Diego appeared, placing sizzling platters of chicken and beef on the table. Abby drew her hands back, fixing a smile on her face as he added the additional pots of guacamole, salsa, sour cream and cheese. The fajitas came in a covered dome to keep them warm. 'Enjoy!' he announced, oblivious to the tension at the table, as he retreated towards the kitchen.

She fixed her eyes on Luke as his eyes took in the spread on the table. Had he been about to say something else? What a terrible burden for a teenage boy, to feel as if he'd let his brother down when he'd needed him most.

She watched as he lifted one of the side plates

and started to ladle food onto it. 'You know it wasn't your fault, right?'

He stopped, a spoonful of salsa between his plate and the serving dish.

'You know that it wasn't your fault you were sick? Anyone can get sick at any time.'

Luke set the spoon down on his plate. Abby had never seen his pale blue eyes so serious. 'I know that the last time I saw my brother I promised him I would teach him how to play poker. I didn't get the chance.'

'But you were a teenager, Luke. You couldn't have known how seriously ill he was.'

'Actually, I could have. I was the one having all the conversations with the doctors. I was the one that saw him on a daily basis and could see the deterioration in his condition. You know what the first words my mother said to me were? *Why didn't you tell me he was so sick?* From my mother!'

Abby took a deep breath. Luke had never really spoken about this before. And she didn't want him to stop. This was good for him. This was good for *them*. The thought came out of nowhere. Why was she thinking about them? There was no them. There hadn't been for five years.

'Luke, your parents should never have left you in that position. As an adult, you must see that now? You must realise how unfair that was.'

He shook his head. 'I don't want to talk about it any more,' he mumbled as he bent to spoon some of the chicken and salsa mixture into his mouth.

A smile crept across her face. In part, to welcome the light relief that was about to come. She watched as the realisation hit Luke as the taste receptors in his mouth went into overdrive. He started to choke and splutter, tears forming in his eyes and streaming down his cheeks.

She pulled his glass over and refilled it with icy water, pushing it towards him and folding her arms across her chest. 'Hot enough for you, Mr Smarty Pants? *I'll have what she's having.*'

Luke covered his mouth with his napkin as he continued to choke, grabbing the glass and drinking thirstily. He thumped it back on the table and eyed her suspiciously. 'You knew, didn't you? You knew exactly how strong it was going to be?'

'I did warn you my tastes have changed. Why do you think Diego brought us a pitcher of iced water?'

His brain went into overdrive. She'd just said it

again, her tastes had changed. Did that mean him? 'I just thought he was being polite. I didn't think he was trying to set me on fire!'

'Do you want me to ask him for something a little milder for you?' The words were like a challenge being thrown down. 'You were the one, after all, who used to say I didn't have the palate for spicy food.'

'No, of course not. This will be fine.' The glint appeared back in his eyes. 'I can out-eat you anywhere. I just need another pitcher of water.'

Abby gave a smile and signalled to Diego. 'Then let the challenge begin.'

CHAPTER SIX

WHEN they got home a very excitable Reuben had crept back out of bed.

Lucy gave a shake of her head. 'I'm sorry, Abby, but he seems to be full of energy tonight.'

Abby smiled. 'Don't worry, Lucy. Thanks for looking after him.'

It took almost an hour to persuade him to get back under the covers. Abby had to read him four stories before he finally nodded off.

By the time she got downstairs Luke had lit the fire in the front room and opened a bottle of wine. Abby slumped down into the nearest armchair and they sat for a few moments in silence, watching the flickering flames.

She took a sip of her wine and studied him carefully. He could still pass for a male model with his surfer-boy looks. There might be a few more lines around his eyes and on his forehead but they didn't detract from his good looks, only added character. She lifted her hand to her face. Did the lines around her eyes add character? Or only make her look older than her thirty years?

She remembered the way that all the females in the hospital where they'd been interns together had flocked around him, batting their eyelids and reapplying their lipstick. And he hadn't shown the slightest bit of interest. In fact, he'd made a point of introducing his girlfriend Abby to them all.

Loyalty had always been Luke's strong point— that and a few other things that took place behind closed doors. She felt the colour rushing into her face at the memories that flooded her mind.

'Penny for your thoughts?'

'What?' Abby gulped. The last thing she wanted to do was share *those* kinds of thoughts with him.

'You looked lost in your thoughts. What's up? Are you tired?'

She leaned back a little further into her chair, hoping he wouldn't notice her reddening cheeks. 'It's certainly been a big day. It's not every day your ex turns up with the First Lady in tow.'

He smiled and nodded slowly. 'I decided to make an entrance.'

'You certainly did.'

Luke set his glass down on the table next to him. 'I honestly nearly died of shock when I saw you sitting there, with your feet on the desk. Good shock, that is. If ever anybody could get me out of a pickle...'

He left the words hanging in the air as he threw a cheeky grin at her.

'I kept expecting someone to jump out from behind a set of curtains with a camera and shout, 'Fooled you'!'

Luke heaved a huge sigh. 'You've no idea how much I wish that had happened.' He pointed to a pile of stuff in the corner. 'What's with the old DVDs and romance novels? I didn't know you were into that.'

'They're for Jennifer Taylor.'

'What?' Luke had just taken another sip of his wine, which he spluttered down the front of his shirt.

'She asked me for them earlier, she's bored out of her mind. I meant to take them along to her...' she glanced at her watch '...but time's just gotten away from me.'

'I'll take them for you.' He looked outside at the

inky-dark night. 'I wouldn't want you walking along that path at this time of night.'

'Which is exactly what I have to do when I'm on call. You don't have to protect me, Luke, I'm a big girl now.'

'I know that.' Something flickered across his mind. 'What happens to Reuben when you're on call?'

'Lucy comes and stays overnight. She uses one of the guest bedrooms.'

He nodded thoughtfully. She'd really thought of everything.

Something twisted inside him again. Why? Reuben just reminded him so much of Ryan. Even some of his little mannerisms had seemed so familiar this evening when he'd been watching him. The way he'd played with that little spiky bit of hair at the front of his head, and the way he'd been so meticulous about lining up his soldiers in a particular order.

So many coincidences, all wrapped up in one little boy.

One little boy that Luke wished was his.

There. He'd thought it. Why was he even thinking like this?

He was hopeless around kids. He'd never really taken the time to get to know any. He wouldn't have a clue how to interact with a child.

Another thought flickered through his head. Was it just the physical similarities? Was it the white-blond hair and blue eyes that was drawing him to Reuben? Was he looking for something he'd lost? A replacement for his brother?

It sent a shiver down his spine.

Then there was the ALL. He'd been there and done that before. There was no way on this earth that he wanted to go through any of that again. He already lost someone who was infinitely precious to him, he just couldn't even contemplate allowing himself to be in that position again.

But what about Abby? The feelings that were resurfacing were making Luke feel alive again for the first time in five years. Did he really want to let her slip through his fingers a second time?

In the space of one day a whole host of possibilities and complications lay in front of him. Things that he'd pushed from his mind for so long. Abby made him happy. She was the key component here. He didn't care about the distance between Washington and Pelican Cove. He cared about what was right in front of him.

But Abby was a package deal. She came with Reuben. And all of this, all of this wasn't about them. It was something that ran much deeper.

This was about finally letting himself think about being a father, something he'd never allowed himself to consider. Something he'd pushed right to the back recesses of his mind, somewhere dark and bleak where things never emerged from.

Now possibilities were floating around in his mind. Tiny, persistent ideas that bounced around, spiralling into something else entirely. Abby had said if she met someone she might have children, or she might adopt again. Would she be happy never to have children of her own?

'Luke? Luke?'

Her voice cut through his thoughts, channelling him back to the present day and time. 'Sorry, what is it?'

'You were lost in a world of your own. I was asking you if you'd brought some scrubs from the hospital to wear tonight.'

He laughed as he remembered her earlier comment about not wearing his 'normal nightwear', which in fact was nothing. 'Don't worry, your son's innocence is safe with me.' He had a twinkle in his eye that she hadn't seen in a long time and it caught her unawares.

Under the flickering firelight Luke's hair stood out and his pale blue eyes captured her gaze and held it, making her breath catch in her throat.

This could be so easy. It would be so simple to step forward into his arms and then step back five years in time. She could almost hear her heart beating against her chest and a low, unfamiliar feeling between her legs. It had been so long since she'd slept with someone. In fact, it had been five long years.

Tears sprang to her eyes in recognition of the thought. Five long years since she'd felt his skin against hers, felt his lips on her throat, her shoulders, her breasts…

She'd been asked out loads of times, on rare occasions she'd agreed to a date and maybe even a kiss. But that had been it. No one had ever lit the flame inside her like Luke had. No one had ever made her want to throw off her clothes and run naked down a beach like Luke had. No one had ever made her want to squeeze into the smallest on-call room in the hospital and barricade the door like Luke had.

Then he was there, right in front of her, kneeling

on the floor in her house, taking the wine glass out of her hand. It was almost like a dream. Almost like a fantasy.

'I miss you, Abby.'

'I've missed you too Luke.'

He ran his hand down her arm, lifting her hand and placing it on his chest. She could feel his beating heart under her fingertips and the rise and fall of his warm chest. After five years Luke was back, right where she'd always wanted him.

She shifted forwards in the chair, her knees naturally easing to the floor in front of him. His hand reached up, catching the side of her face and pulling her towards him. And he kissed her. Slowly and gently, as she felt his heartbeat quicken under her palm.

She wanted to touch him. She wanted to feel his skin on hers, so with trembling hands she started to undo the buttons on his shirt, slowly at first, never moving her lips from his, then tugged at them in frustration as they halted her progress. His kiss had deepened, his tongue easing its way into her mouth. His hands slid under her light cardigan and she lifted her arms upwards as he pulled it off in one seamless movement.

His hand stroked across her face as he pulled backwards to watch her in the flickering firelight. 'You're so beautiful, Abby,' he whispered as he ran his fingers along her jaw line and down the delicate skin on her throat. She caught her breath. She knew what was coming next.

His hands met at her breastbone then separated outwards towards her aching nipples. He brushed against them, making her feel as if they were on fire. A smile danced across his lips. 'So what would you like me to do, Abby?'

He slid the straps on her summer dress down over her shoulders. She inhaled sharply as he bent his head down lower, releasing the clip on her bra and catching her nipple in his teeth. Abby could feel the throb between her legs. His tongue danced over her nipple. 'This?' he asked, his pale blue eyes glinting wickedly.

'Oh, yes,' she whispered. Her hands reached around his back and pulled him even closer. This was meant to be a kiss. This was meant to be just an *I've-missed-you* kiss. But she wanted so much more.

Luke lifted the scatter cushions from the chair she'd been sitting on and placed them on the rug beneath them. He laid her down gently as he positioned himself above her. This was what he'd wanted from the moment he'd seen her that morning. He bent his head and blew on her nipples, causing her to arch her back towards him. 'Oh, Luke,' she moaned.

He slid his hand under her dress, pushing aside her panties and plunging his finger into the wet moistness. She lifted her hips towards him, urging him to plunge deeper. 'These clothes have got to go, Abby,' he said, as in one movement he reached up his hands and yanked down her panties, pulling them over her slim legs and feet. She wiggled her way out of her dress and threw it onto the nearby sofa.

She tugged at the belt on his trousers. 'You're right, these clothes have definitely got to go.'

It only took a few seconds to undo his belt and reveal the white shorts she'd admired earlier. Even in the dim light, they couldn't possibly conceal, or contain, his stiff erection. She ran her fingers along the length, smiling as she heard his sharp intake of breath. She wrapped her arms around his neck, whispering in his ear, 'I guess all the clothes should really go—no matter how nice they are.'

Her hands slid down his back, cupping his buttocks. Her legs had naturally separated, allowing him to fit between them. All he had to do was…

'Wait a minute!' Abby leapt upwards. 'Condoms, we need condoms.' She barely noticed the surprise on his face as her naked body ran out the door and up the stairs.

Luke was frozen. Why would she need condoms? After all, he couldn't make her pregnant, could he? What else did she need protection against?

He lay on his side, in front of the fire, his head leaning on his hand. Abby dashed back into the room at top speed, clutching a box in her hands. She stood in front of him, completely naked, biting her bottom lip. 'I think they might be out of date,' she mumbled.

His eyes drifted up and down the length of her body. Her creamy skin illuminated by the dancing firelight. She was still perfection. In his previous visions, Abby had always reminded him of Rapunzel with her long flowing locks. But the new, shorter, edgier hairstyle suited her. It revealed more of her body, in particular her luscious full breasts and flaring hips. His eyes fell even lower, to the blonde triangle of hair.

'Come here.' His voice was deep, husky.

She walked towards him and knelt down, the box still in her hand.

He took it, an amused gleam in his eye, and glanced at the date. 'I guess they're not going to be much use.'

Somehow, the fact that Abby had a box of out-of-date condoms sent good sensations running through him. He bent forward, taking one of her nipples into his mouth and gently teasing it with his teeth. 'So it's been a long time, then, Abby?'

She nodded wordlessly. Her mind was too en-grossed by his actions to formulate a response.

'Would it help if I told you it had been a long time for me too?'

Her eyes widened. He remembered her questions about 'Luscious Lisa' earlier. Did she think he'd slept with her? He closed his hands around the box before tossing it carelessly to one side. 'You're safe, Abby. I'm safe. Now let's see what we can do about making up for the last five years.' He rolled onto his back, pulling her above him. 'I think the lady should be in control,' he teased huskily.

'I think I can do that.' She poised above him, hovering over his thick length, then bent forward, her hair brushing over his chest as she kissed him thoroughly, before lowering herself gently down on him.

The sensation was immediate. Fullness. A feeling that spread through her whole body, like a pulsating heat generating outwards. It felt like coming home.

But Luke wasn't finished with her yet. He started to move, rhythmically, playing a tune that he hadn't played in years. He knew exactly where to touch her, where to stroke and how to take her right to the edge. And so he did. Again. And again. And again.

Abby woke at seven a.m. The sun was streaming through the curtains, showing the start of a beautiful sun-kissed day. She stretched in her comfortable bed. Then she realised something was wrong. The house was silent. Her house was never silent at this time in the morning. But, then, she never slept this late, and she never woke up alone. Reuben always woke up in the middle of the night and she brought him into bed beside her.

She sat up in bed and rubbed her eyes. She couldn't even remember how she had got to bed. The last thing she remembered she'd been lying on the rug in the living room with Luke. The memories made her blush.

Abby threw back the cover, pushed her feet into her slippers and grabbed her dressing gown from the foot of the bed. As soon as she pushed open her bedroom door she could hear voices. Happy voices. No, Reuben's voice was happy—Luke's voice was a little strained. She wandered along the corridor towards them.

Luke was lying in the guest bedroom, propped up on some pillows. Somehow he'd resisted coming into bed alongside her. He must have known she wouldn't have wanted Reuben to see them in bed together. His duvet had been transformed into an assault course for a variety of soldiers and cars. Ornaments, toothbrushes and aerosol cans littered the cover and Reuben was having the time of his life. *Crash! Bang!*

'Give me the red one, Luke, it's the supercharged one. You take the blue one—it can fly. Now, ready, set, go!'

Abby stood in the doorway. They hadn't even noticed her yet. She could feel the butterflies in her stomach. This was the man that didn't want children. Ever.

Hell, he hadn't even liked coming up to the paediatric ward to pick her up and on the few occasions that he had appeared, he hadn't been able to get out of the place quickly enough.

Then something else struck her. She'd never seen Reuben do this before. He'd never had a male adult role model in his life. Most of his adult contacts were with Abby or Lucy. She watched him as he leapt onto Luke's back and tried to tumble him to the floor.

She frowned. It was much more rough and tumble behaviour than he did with her. Was this what a little boy needed? And he wasn't getting it from her?

For the first time ever she felt strangely lacking. Maybe Reuben needed more than her?

'Abby, hi.' Luke's voice cut through her thoughts. His eyes were heavy from lack of sleep and an uncomfortable smile was on his face. 'Reuben woke me early this morning. He decided we would be playmates.'

Luke shifted underneath the cover, causing numerous items to move around the bed.

'Wow, Luke, now we've got a mountain!' shouted Reuben as he pounced on Luke's bent knee.

Luke lifted his eyebrows at Abby. 'Does he wake this early every day?'

Abby nodded solemnly.

Luke swallowed thoughtfully. Long, comfortable lie-ins were obviously a thing from the past in this household. The kind of thing he used to do with Abby on a morning like this. Long, lazy days usually spent wrapped in each other's arms with no one else to think about. If only. He caught the expression on her face. He could tell she was uncomfortable, but why?

It was time to get her mind on other things. 'This morning we have the car and soldier extraordinaire assault course. Would you care to have a try?' He lifted the corner of the duvet cover and gave her a wink. Abby he could deal with. Abby he was comfortable with.

She watched, an uneasy feeling spreading over her. *Her child*. Reuben was hers. And he had been right from the start. Hers alone. She didn't have to share him. What's more, she didn't *want* to share him.

'Are you coming in, Mommy?'

She shook her head. 'No, honey. Let's go downstairs and make breakfast.'

In one leap, Reuben flew across the room and flung himself into her arms. 'Great, I'm starving.' The warmth of his little body spread that familiar feeling throughout her body. The feeling that gave her reassurance of her place and role in his life. She was his mother. No one could take that away from her. 'What are we having, Mommy?'

'What do you want?'

'Porridge! Porridge is my favouwite!'

Abby gave him a kiss on the cheek and set him down on the floor. 'Then porridge it is.' She turned her head towards Luke. 'And Dr Luke will get dressed before he comes downstairs,' she said determinedly. The thought of Luke parading around her kitchen in his thin theatre scrubs conjured up butterflies in her stomach that she didn't need.

Abby started as the phone rang as she walked by the hall table. She picked it up quickly and listened to the voice at the other end. Luke was wandering down the stairs towards her, some decidedly rumpled clothes in place and his hair standing on end.

'Yes, yes. No, I understand.' She winked at Luke as he appeared behind her. 'Oh, don't worry, I'm sure I can find *someone* to do that. No problem, see you later.'

'Who was that?'

'David Fairgreaves.'

'What? Is something wrong with Jennifer Taylor?'

She shook her head. 'No, Jennifer Taylor is doing fine. No signs of going into labour as yet. Valerie Carter, however, has just decided to go into an early labour.'

Luke's brow furrowed. 'Who's Valerie Carter?'

'Do you remember that yesterday I told you our cardiologist was 38 weeks pregnant, with a full clinic?'

He nodded. 'So that's Valerie Carter.' The realisation of her words had just struck him. 'So what have you just volunteered me for?'

'Just to cover her clinics and procedures tomorrow.' She gave a little smile over her shoulder as she walked towards the kitchen. 'Let's face it, you don't have anything else to do for the next few days.'

Luke gave her a lazy smile. 'True. It's not like I can do anything for Jennifer Taylor. I might as well make myself useful. But I thought you said

you only had a few deliveries a year?' He followed
her into the kitchen and as she washed her hands
at the sink, he stepped up behind her, sliding his
arms around her waist and pressing the full length
of his body against hers. She leaned backwards
into him, and his head dropped to the exposed
skin at the nape of her neck as he started to run
some butterfly-like kisses up to the back of her
ear.

'It's true, but what's that old saying, "When it
rains, it pours"?'

He could hear her breath catching in her throat,
knowing the effect he was having on her. 'So I'm
going to spend the next few days surrounded by
babies, then?' His voice was low and husky and
there was a certain something awakening behind
her as he pressed closer.

Abby let out a little groan as she answered, leaning her head further back and exposing even more
of the white skin on her neck. 'Looks like it. Time
to get used to it, Luke. Pelican Cove is a small
place, you can't just hide away because you don't
like kids.' Her voice was loaded, her tone almost
accusing.

'You don't like kids, Dr Luke?' Reuben's voice

was like a bolt out of the blue, causing them to spring apart.

He pulled his T-shirt lower to cover the swell in his trousers. Damn! He'd forgotten all about Reuben. All he'd thought about was Abby and what he wanted to do to her. The intrusion irked him. He wasn't used to this. He wasn't used to being mindful of small eyes and ears. He was used to walking across his apartment wearing nothing but his birthday suit. And previously, when he'd been with Abby, they'd managed to christen every room in the apartment they'd shared. How could you do that with a child about? It was bad enough to be woken early every day, without any extracurricular activities being interrupted as well.

Reuben's voice was full of astonishment. 'Why don't you like kids?'

Luke shifted uncomfortably as a tinge of red appeared on his cheeks. 'Who said I don't like kids?'

'My mom did.' His eyes were large and his expression solemn. 'And she knows everything. Don't you like me?' There was something in the way he said it, like a four-year-old who implicitly trusted his own little world, that tugged at Luke's heartstrings. He wanted the floor to open up and swallow him. For a second, he'd almost wished the little guy away. He was the adult here, and he was a guest in their home. It was up to him to make an effort. Reuben was part of Abby's life, and whether he liked it or not he was going to have to get used to the idea.

A picture flitted through his mind. A picture of another little boy on a day out at the beach— wide-eyed, expressive and trusting—just before his wretch of a big brother had dunked him in a rock pool.

He could feel Abby's eyes staring at him, burrowing into the side of his face. He bent downwards and whispered in Reuben's ear, 'Of course I like you, Reuben. You look just like another little boy that I used to play with. And I liked him—a lot.'

Reuben's eyes narrowed, before he nodded acceptingly and trotted off to play.

Luke breathed a sigh of relief and sagged back against the wall. This was tougher than he'd thought.

CHAPTER SEVEN

ABBY headed out to the front step, shaking some crumbs from the breakfast tablecloth. Luke couldn't remember the last time he'd seen someone use a fabric tablecloth—it must be one of the things her aunt had left.

'So what are we going to do today?' There was a twinkle in his eye. He could think of lots of things he'd like to do with Abby today.

'*We*—' she emphasized the word strongly as she looked pointedly at Reuben '—were going to do a little shopping, then head down to the beach.'

Luke glanced downwards at his rumpled clothes—a fine cotton shirt and dress trousers—not exactly made for the beach. He grimaced as he thought of the contents of his suitcase—more shirts, suits and ties. Clothes designed to wear at a professional conference to impress. No casual clothes at all. Certainly nothing suitable for a beach.

He turned his head towards the ocean view outside. The early sunrise sent shimmers of pink and orange glistening across the cove waters. It was going to be a gorgeous day.

'Think you can manage to spend the day with a family, bachelor boy?' It was a loaded question and Abby didn't wait for his response but turned on her heel and headed back into the kitchen.

Luke watched her retreating back, in her figure-hugging shorts and skimpy T-shirt. He could only imagine what she'd look like in a bikini. It was a sight he didn't want to miss.

'You bet,' he murmured as he followed her indoors.

An hour later they were in one of the local stores. Abby flicked through the rails. 'Nope, nope, no, no…' She gave him a cursory glance as the clothes hangers practically skidded along the rails. 'Ahh, this one.' She held up a purple T-shirt and tossed it in his direction with a nod of approval, before moving over to the clothes stand with stacks of folded shorts.

Luke shook his head in bewilderment at the mirror, as he held the T-shirt up in front of him.

He gave a little smile. The colouring and style were perfect for him, he squinted at the label— yes, it was the right size, the woman hadn't lost her touch.

He heard a loud sigh at his feet. Reuben was sitting on the floor, bucket and spade in hand, looking extremely bored. 'She does this with me too.'

'Does what?'

'Picks all my clothes.' He shook his little blond head. 'It's best not to argue or we'll be here *for ever*.'

Luke let out a roar of laughter. Spoken like a man who knew which battles to fight. Reuben screwed up his nose as he stared at Luke's purple T-shirt, 'She usually picks good stuff. You should be okay.'

'Okay for what?' Abby appeared at their sides, clutching two pairs of knee-length shorts in her hands. She pointed towards the nearby chang-ing room. 'Go and make sure these fit,' she said, thrusting the shorts in his direction.

He raised his eyebrow at her. 'What's wrong, Abs, worried you've forgotten what size I am?'

She rolled her eyes at his innuendo-laden question, before giving him a naughty smile of her own. 'Heads up, little guy.' She tapped Reuben on the shoulder. 'I've decided that you can pick Luke's swimwear.'

She pointed towards a rail loaded with various styles of swimming shorts and trunks. Luke gulped. The neon bright colors were already hurting his eyes from a distance.

'Cool,' mumbled Reuben, before heading over towards the rail.

'You don't mind—do you, Luke?'

He shook his head quickly before ducking inside the changing room. 'Please, please, don't let it be the tiny trunks,' he muttered as he pushed his legs into the shorts Abby had picked for him. In less than thirty seconds he was done. Both sets of shorts were perfect for the beach, loose fitting and ending just above his knees.

He stuck his head back out the changing room. 'The shorts are fine, but do I only get one T-sh—' He stopped. Abby had already picked out another two T-shirts for him. She stared down at his long legs. 'The shorts are nice...' she smiled '...but we really need to do something about those shoes.'

Luke laughed and followed her gaze. Beach shorts and black leather Italian shoes really didn't mix.

'I've found you the best pair of *swimmers* ever, Luke!' Reuben rushed over, holding the brightly coloured shorts in front of him. 'Whaddya think?'

Luke lifted them from his small hands. Just as he'd feared. Bright green neon ninja turtles. The little face was staring up at him, so pleased with the item that he'd found. Waiting for him to say something.

Abby frowned as she reached over and fingered the swim shorts. 'These look just like yours, Reuben.'

'I know!' he shouted. 'We'll be a match! Isn't that cool?'

Luke's eyes drifted between Reuben and Abby. He couldn't read the expression on her face. It was almost as if she wasn't quite sure how to react, what to say. Not like Abby at all. But he could read the expression on Reuben's face and he didn't hesitate.

'These look fabulous, Reuben. I love them.'

'You do?'

'Sure I do. Now give me two minutes so I can pay for all this stuff.'

Luke pulled the labels off the T-shirt and shorts that he was wearing and handed them to the cashier, along with the other items.

Two minutes later they left with his crumpled shirt and dress trousers stuffed into one of the plastic bags.

Abby ran her eyes up and down the length of him. Something prickled under her gaze. Something thankfully hidden beneath baggy beach shorts. She knew him better than he knew himself.

Another hour later they were on the beach, lying on their matching ninja turtle beach towels. Luke pulled off his newly purchased sneakers and exposed his hot feet to the cool air around them.

'You didn't have to do that.'

'Do what?'

She stuck the parasol into the sand and tilted it towards Reuben's towel to shade him from the sun. 'Buy all this stuff.' She pointed to the items lying around them.

Luke leaned towards her. 'I'll have you know

that I've always wanted a ninja turtle towel. They just didn't seem to have them anywhere in Washington.' He lay back, raising his hands to shade his face from the sun. 'I guess I just lucked out, coming here.'

'I guess you did.'

The words seemed to hang in the air between them, the meaning more than either one could say. Abby bit her bottom lip. Today was so different for her. Usually when she and Reuben came to the beach, they came alone. But Luke's presence was everywhere, and it wasn't just his muscular frame.

She'd noticed a difference in Reuben, how he was acting. He kept giving sidelong glances at Luke, looking for his approval on what towel he wanted, what ice cream he picked, what path they chose to walk to the beach.

And it was uncomfortable. She was used to being the centre of Reuben's whole world—as he was hers—and something about this just didn't feel right. She wasn't used to him asking someone else's opinion or considering someone else's point of view. She made all the decisions for the two of them. It was her word that was law. Her hand that he held. Her permission that he sought.

Abby gave herself a shake. This was silly. Luke was only here for a few days. He was a novelty to Reuben, a novelty that would soon wear off when Reuben realised that Luke wasn't really interested in him.

Her eyes drifted over to the water's edge. Reuben had met some other kids and was busy making mud pies—his favorite hobby every time they came here. Pelican Cove was lucky, they had life-guards who patrolled the beach during the summer season, both for the families and for the ardent surfers who spent most of the day on the waves.

There were lots of families here, all resting back and enjoying their time at the beach.

Families.

Something about the word made her uncomfort-able again. She cast her eyes around the beach. Would other people think they were a family? A happy mom, dad and son spending a day at the beach?

Her eyes fell on Luke as he leaned back with his eyes closed on the towel. With his white-blond hair and matching swimwear it was likely that people would assume he was Reuben's father. She bit her lip.

But he wasn't. And he hadn't wanted to be. He hadn't wanted to be a father to any child. So why was he here playing happy families with her today?

Abby gave a sigh and leaned back against her towel. There was no point in thinking about this. There was no point in over-analysing things. What was done was done. In a few days' time Luke would be gone again. So maybe she should just focus on the good. The companionship. The warmth, the comfort and the passion. It could be a long time before she felt those things again.

Luke was dreaming. Or maybe it was daydreaming. The sun was beating down on his skin and if he just turned on his side and reached out there was a warm body next to his. A warm body that arched, then fitted comfortably next to his, sliding into place as if it was always meant to be there, easing tight butt cheeks right against his...

'Luke!'

The enthusiastic voice pulled him from the wonderland he'd been inhabiting, jerking him back to present day and time. Or maybe he hadn't been dreaming. His body was spooned around Abby's, his hand wrapped tightly around her waist. Now, if he just lifted his hand a little more and slipped it underneath her shirt...

'Come on, Luke!'

The voice was still there and wasn't going to go away. Luke heaved himself up, pulling his shorts to adjust their position. He blinked in the bright sunlight and pulled his shades down from his forehead. Abby was sleeping peacefully on the beach towel next to him. She hadn't even heard Reuben's voice.

Luke tried to crowd out the immediate thoughts in his head. The thoughts that tried to vanquish this little guy from sight. He stared at the little pair of eyes fixed on his. Nope. He definitely wasn't going away.

'What's up, Reuben?'

'I want to go in the water and I'm not allowed without an adult. Beach rules number one.' The words rolled off his tongue in ease.

Luke's face broke into a smile. How could he fail to? He leaned forward. 'So how many beach rules are there, Reuben?'

'Seven.' He didn't hesitate for a second. 'Wanna hear them all?'

Luke nodded slowly as he glanced at Abby

again. She looked tired and he'd kept her up half the night. She deserved some rest. He pulled the beach parasol closer to shade her from the sun and stood up. 'Let's go, little guy.'

He hesitated, just for a second, before reaching out his hand to Reuben's and walking down to the water's edge with him. Around them he could see lots of families in the water, fathers throwing their kids over their shoulders and ducking them under the waves. How hard could this be?

'I want to do that.' Reuben's voice had a determined edge to it, his finger pointing in the direction of the surfers.

Luke's brow furrowed. Right now, he'd like to do that too.

'Have you done it before, short stuff?'

'Mommy can't surf. She said I'd need to wait for one of her friends to show me.'

Luke nodded. Sounded reasonable enough. There was a shack on the beach where some guy was hiring out surfboards, boogie boards and life vests. He pulled Reuben over and fitted him with a bright orange life vest. His eyes ran over the boards on offer and settled on a purple one. He pointed towards it. 'We'll take that one.'

SCARLET WILSON   175

'Really?' Reuben's eyes widened at the adult-sized board, full of enthusiasm and excitement.

'Sure.' Luke pulled some dollar bills from his pocket and handed them over before lifting the board under his arm and walking down towards the ocean. He bent to speak to Reuben before entering the ocean.

'So, I've got some ocean rules for you.'

Reuben nodded solemnly whilst his eyes swept over the ocean in front of him. He was practically jumping for joy.

'First time out, we're just going to paddle the board out a little, sitting on it together. Got it?'

Reuben nodded. 'I'm going to surf,' he said proudly.

Luke raised his finger. 'We won't be doing any of the standing-up stuff yet. And we won't be going too far out either.' He put his arms out, his body drifting from one side to the other. 'We're just going to get a feel for the waves, okay?'

'Let's go, Luke.' Reuben was bouncing on the tips of his toes. He could hardly wait to start. A wide smile broke across Luke's face. He knew another guy who used to be exactly the same.

He set the board down and plopped Reuben astride on top of it, pushing it out into the waves until the water reached his waist. Then he pulled himself up next to Reuben, sitting close behind him, and leaned forward. 'Let's start paddling!' he shouted.

And then they started. Paddling their hands as fast as they could, pushing themselves out towards the wide ocean expanse. After a few minutes they stopped and turned the board round to face the shoreline. And sat there—feeling the waves.

And Reuben chatted. Constantly. And asked questions. Constantly. For a four-year-old he seemed to have spent some considerable time watching National Geographic. He wanted to talk about tides and moons. And crabs and dolphins. And sharks. Mainly about sharks. Before he moved onto volcanoes then racing cars.

And Luke listened. And listened. This four-year-old stuff wasn't as hard as it seemed. He was just a mini-version of Ryan. He had the same boundless energy and enthusiasm—they must have paddled in and out around ten times by now and his brain never stopped.

Reuben wanted to know everything. The kid was just like a giant sponge, trying to soak up every bit of information all around him. And if

Luke could have transported himself through time and space to a time when Ryan had still been alive, he knew that they would still end up here, in this place. Because everything about this just felt so right. On these surfboards, at this beach, enjoying everything the day had to offer.

They turned to face the shore again and Luke squinted. It looked as if Abby had woken up. 'Look, short stuff, there's your mom, looking for us.' He pointed to her bikini-clad figure on the beach. A very small red bikini that made him wish he was much closer to shore.

'Uh-oh.'

'What do you mean—uh-oh?'

'Mom's gonna be mad.'

'Why would she be mad?'

Reuben gave a little chuckle. A tiny four-year-old-sized chuckle. 'Cos I'm not allowed.'

Luke felt his stomach sink. 'Reuben Tyler, you're not allowed to do what, exactly?'

'Surf.'

Luke caught sight of Abby as she walked swiftly toward the shoreline. She was not in a happy place. He leaned forward on the board. 'Start paddling, little man, looks like we're in trouble.'

* * *

Abby had woken with a start. She never fell asleep on the beach. Not when she was there with Reuben. That was irresponsible. Anything could happen.

Silence. All around her. Well, not completely. There were still plenty of other families on the beach, digging sandcastles, eating snacks. But there was a strange silence around her. One that she wasn't used to.

She sat up quickly, her hand reaching over to the towel next to her. It was cold. No warm body had just vacated it. Her head flicked from side to side, trying to catch a glimpse of either pair of neon green turtle shorts on the beach. Nowhere. They were nowhere in sight.

Her heart gave a little lurch. Stop it. Reuben wasn't alone. He must be with Luke. But where were they?

She saw the kids to her left that Reuben had made the mud pies with earlier. Pulling her hat firmly on her head, she walked towards them quickly. 'Have you seen Reuben lately?' she asked, trying to keep the strain from her voice.

The kids barely looked upwards. Both were too immersed in burying something in the sand. 'He's surfing with his dad,' came the reply.

Her head shot upwards, eyes flickering over the horizon. She could see lots of surfboards on the ocean, most of them far away, like specks on the waves. He couldn't have. He wouldn't have.

Then she saw it. A board nearer the shore with a hand, raised giving her a wave. Two bodies sitting one in front of the other astride the surfboard, paddling towards her. The two white-blond heads close together, laughing and paddling as fast as they could.

She ran down towards the shoreline as the purple board bobbed towards her. Her eyes couldn't even focus on Luke. She looked entirely at Reuben.

'Reuben Tyler, what do you think you're doing?'

'Paddling,' Reuben answered, and Luke almost guffawed. Lord, this kid was smart.

'Get off that board right now. You know you're not allowed to go surfing.'

'Surfing's the next lesson, Mommy. Today Luke and I were just feeling the waves.' He held his arms out and rocked his body from side to side like Luke had done earlier.

Abby felt her heart pounding in her chest. She waded into the water and yanked Reuben from the board, putting his feet down firmly on solid ground. Her face was pale. 'He's not allowed to do things like this, Luke. It's too dangerous. I won't let Reuben take risks.'

Luke slid off the board and pulled it to shore. He placed his hand on Abby's arm. 'He was perfectly safe with me, Abby. I wouldn't take risks with your son.'

She met his eyes and swallowed hard. What she really wanted to do was shout and scream at him for taking her son out onto the ocean. She could see the bright orange life preserver wrapped around him, but right now she didn't care. Anything could have happened. They could have been swept away. The tide could have turned, a current could have caught them or a rip-tide. A visible shudder swept down her spine.

A hand crept around her waist and a warm, wet body touched hers. Reuben was already bounding up the beach towards their parasol and towels.

'He's fine Abby.' The breath from the words tickled the side of her neck. She watched the retreating figure. He was fine. He was safe.

So why was she so wound up? Was it the other kids, calling Luke Reuben's dad? Or was it the thought of Reuben getting to do something special, something he'd asked to do for a long time, with someone other than her? The thoughts spun around in her head. Was it possible she was jealous of the connection Reuben and Luke were making? A connection that didn't include her?

Abby pulled her white cardigan a little closer around her shoulders. It had taken longer than normal to get Reuben to sleep tonight. He'd been so excited by his day at the beach he'd been chattering for hours. She looked at the little sleeping figure in the bed in front of her. His hair lay on the blue pillow, his chest rising and falling lightly with every breath. Perfect. And hers.

She sighed and closed the door quietly behind her. Luke had said he would sort out dinner. He'd been tiptoeing around her for the last few hours. Probably trying to placate her after her outburst on the beach. Had she been unreasonable? She'd never had to consult anyone else on her parenting of Reuben. She'd thought she was all that Reuben would ever need. But as her son was getting older was that still the case? Or did a little boy really need a father figure in his life?

The smell of food was drifting along the corridor. She went down the stairs and into the kitchen but there was no sign of Luke. A light breeze caught her dress and made it dance around her legs, and she turned swiftly. The front door was open.

Luke was sitting on a picnic rug on the grass in front of her house. He smiled as she came down the steps and handed her a glass of chilled wine. 'Cheers,' he said, clinking the glass with his bottle of beer as she sat down beside him.

'I thought we shouldn't let this beautiful evening go to waste.'

A smile crept across her lips. Two plates of barbeque chicken and baked potatoes sat in front of her. Last time they'd eaten this meal, it had come from a take-out and they'd been sitting on top of a hill in Washington, watching the sunset. This time Luke had obviously spent some time mastering her outside barbeque. The smell was mouthwatering.

'I wonder where you got this idea. This seems awfully familiar,' she murmured as she saw the glint in his eye.

'I wonder indeed,' he replied as he gently ran a hand along her bare leg. 'So what do you think?'

She gave him a little smile as the nerve endings in her skin caused her hairs to stand on end. She looked down at the plates. 'I think your cooking skills have obviously improved over the last few years. But I'm a bit scared to ask who taught you.'

He leaned back onto one elbow and gave her a flirty smile. 'I'm self-taught. You left me with one saucepan and a microwave. What's a guy to do?'

He moved a little closer, slipping an arm around her shoulders as he lifted one of the plates onto her lap. 'And that wasn't what I meant.'

'What did you mean, then?' Somehow she knew exactly how this night was going to turn out. She took a bite of the barbeque chicken and gave a deep sigh. She couldn't remember the last time someone had cooked for her. Right now it didn't matter what Luke had served—anything would have been delicious.

He gestured towards the view in front of them. The sun was just beginning to set, sending deep oranges and red spilling across the ocean waves.

'Washington or Pelican Cove, which has the best sunset?'

She spluttered as she took a drink from her wine

glass. 'How can you even ask that question? When did we ever get views like this in Washington?'

Luke took a drink from his beer bottle and leaned downwards, whispering in her ear. 'I guess you're right. The ocean view here is a clear winner.' He took the plate from her hands and set it down on the grass next to them. Abby leaned back on her elbows, a smile across her face as Luke's body crossed over hers, his hands on either side of her head, his body right above hers. 'But there's a view here that I'd much rather see.' He bent forward and she tipped her head backwards, exposing the white skin at her throat again as he pushed her cardigan to one side and started to kiss the delicate skin.

Her heart fluttered. He still knew exactly where to touch her. How to connect with her. How to send her pulse racing at the slightest touch. 'And what view might that be, Dr Storm?'

He gave a deep, throaty laugh at the use of his title. She'd reverted back to their game-playing from years ago, when they'd both just qualified and been eager to use their titles. His head bent lower, inching her coral-coloured sundress away from her breasts. His heavy-lidded eyes met hers and he growled, 'What do you think, Dr Tyler?'

She wrapped her arms around his neck, running her fingers through his short hair and then down the wide planes of his back, settling her hands on his butt cheeks and pulling him closer to her. Her legs opened naturally, letting him settle into the space between them as he pressed closer. She could feel exactly what she wanted.

Something about this was perfect. Five years ago, on a secluded Washington hill, they'd been in exactly this same position. His mouth tickled lower, pushing her bra aside and catching her nipple between his teeth. She let out a sharp gasp and thrust her hips against his.

There had been something about this before. Being out in the open air, at sunset in a place where no one could find them. This time they were on her front lawn, but her house was at the end of a secluded path that no one came down. She heard the sound of a zipper being released and felt him nudge her panties to one side.

There was wicked gleam in his eye. 'So, Dr Tyler, since we're re-creating a moment from our past, do you want to re-create the full evening or just part of the evening?'

It was a loaded question. The night in question

had been long and eventful. She nibbled at his earlobe. 'I was with a younger model then,' she murmured. 'I'm a little concerned the older version won't be able to keep up.'

She felt a tickle at her throat as his evening stubble scraped her skin. His voice was heavy with desire. 'Oh, no, this isn't the older version, this is the new, improved version. With power settings.'

'Is that right?' She could feel his fingers, easing into her and taking her towards the place she wanted to be. 'Let's see these power settings, then.'

Her hips tilted upwards, readying herself for him.

'Mommy!' Her body stiffened instinctively. 'Mommy, where are you?'

Luke groaned and rolled off her as she scrabbled to pull her clothing back into place. She leaned forward and dropped a kiss on his forehead. 'Sorry, Luke, the joys of motherhood.' She jumped up and ran up the steps inside the house. 'I'm right here, honey.'

He heard her trying to placate the little boy who'd obviously woken suddenly, and he heaved a sigh, straining to adjust his zipper back into place.

It would be a long time before she was back. *If* she came back.

Luke picked up his half-full beer bottle and took a long, hard swig. Pelican Cove was a gorgeous setting but it came with complications. Complications that he didn't know if he could handle. Everything about Abby was perfect and the connection between them was still there. The chemistry. When they were together he felt complete. Something he hadn't felt at any point in the last five years. Something he'd never managed to capture with anyone else.

But could he live like this? With constant interruptions? No more long lie-ins, no more lazy days in bed, with just themselves to worry about.

For a few hours that afternoon he'd thought he could. He felt something towards Reuben. The little boy had hung on his every word. Wanted to impress him. Wanted to spend time with him.

But the question remained. *Did* he want to spend time with Reuben?

CHAPTER EIGHT

ABBY watched in wonder at the huge array of equipment being unloaded in the ambulance bay. All this for one baby?

She caught sight of a familiar face at the back of one of the crates. 'Linc!' she shouted, as she pushed her way through the jumble of people.

Lincoln Adams was the neonatologist she usually worked with at San Francisco Children's Hospital. She gave him a quick hug and led him inside the emergency department.

'Are you okay, Linc? You look really tired.'

He shook his head, his hands on his hips. 'Let's just say a certain man…' his eyes followed James Turner as he strode through the department '…appeared at my door at 3 a.m. yesterday morning and told me I had to come to Pelican Cove. I haven't slept in two days.' He ran his fingers through his short, spiky hair. 'He wouldn't take no for an answer.'

Abby nodded. 'I know exactly how you feel. I'm really sorry, Linc. He asked me for the best neonatologist that I knew. And you were the natural answer.'

Lincoln leaned over and gave her a hug, obvious fatigue making him hold the position a little longer than necessary. 'It's not your fault, Abby.'

'Want to introduce me?' Luke's voice made Abby jump.

'Yes, sure.' She noticed the amused expression on Linc's face. 'Lincoln Adams, this is Luke Storm, he's the President's cardiologist and unfortunately for him he's the only doctor at the moment to have met the security protocols required to treat the President's family.' Lincoln held out his hand towards Luke and the two men shook hands briefly, each sizing the other up. 'Luke, this is Lincoln Adams, the best neonatologist at San Francisco Children's Hospital. He'll be the man looking after our imminent arrival.'

Luke eyed up the new recruit suspiciously. Was there a reason he'd been so keen to hang onto Abby? She may have had an out-of-date box of condoms in Pelican Cove, but what about her home in San Francisco? Was there something more to this relationship?

Lincoln Adams pulled uncomfortably at his crumpled T-shirt. 'Is there somewhere I can get changed, Abby? And somewhere we can get our equipment set up? I want to make sure that we are ready.'

Abby gave a quick nod. 'We've designated a room for you...' she rolled her eyes '...and all your equipment. Have you brought some extra staff?'

Lincoln gave a quick nod.

'That's great. I'll also assign one of our NPs to your team to familiarise you all with the surroundings. Come with me and I'll show you where the room is and you can let your staff start to unpack.' She placed her hand firmly at the small of his back. 'In the meantime, you look like death warmed over. I'll show you where you can shower and change, and then I'll take you for something to eat with David Fairgreaves. It'll give the two of you a chance to discuss your patient.'

Lincoln nodded gratefully. 'You do know that's the only reason I came here, right? The chance to work with David Fairgreaves was too good an opportunity to miss.'

'And the fact you've looked after the First Baby won't be too shoddy on your résumé either, will it?'

Lincoln shook his head and the two of them walked down the corridor together, leaving Luke with an uncomfortable feeling twisting around inside him. What was this? Why did he feel uneasy about the relaxed relationship Abby obviously had with her professional colleague? Wasn't it just what he would expect from her?

He was sure that Lincoln Adams looked and felt exactly the same as he did. Like a fish out of water. In a strange place, with strange people and patients he didn't know.

Luke glanced at the piece of paper he had clutched in his hand. The list of cardiac patients he'd seen that morning at the clinic. Everything had been straightforward, easy almost. He'd been assigned a secretary and a nurse that morning who'd sorted out every test he'd ordered or prescription that he'd written for the patients. This place ran like clockwork and it made him a little envious of his overloaded clinic back in Washington.

He wandered back through to the emergency room.

'Dr Luke!'

Lucy, Reuben's childcare worker, came careering through the doors towards him. 'Oh, thank God it's you,' she gasped as she sat Reuben down on the worktop of the reception desk. Reuben was crying at the top of his voice, holding his arm outwards away from his body. 'He cut his hand, playing on the beach.' She glanced over her shoulder. 'Is Abby here?'

Luke shook his head. 'She's just taken one of the new doctors through to the other side of the hospital.' He looked down at the red-faced child and shook off his feelings of unease. He could do this. He was a professional. 'So what do we have here?'

He gently lifted the handkerchief that was held tightly on Reuben's hand and assessed the damage in an instant, lifting Reuben up into his arms and signalling for Lucy to follow.

'We'll go through to one of the suture rooms,' he said quickly. 'Can you give Dr Tyler a page please and tell her to come back to the ER?' he asked one of the receptionists.

The woman gave him a quick nod and picked up the nearest phone.

Luke placed Reuben on the bed in the suture room, pulling one of the angled lights a little closer. He quickly set up a trolley and scrubbed his hands under the sink, before putting on some gloves and opening the sterile suture pack. Lucy kept her arm around Reuben, whispering in his ear and pointing out the characters painted on the walls.

'So what happened, Lucy?'

She shook her head. 'He wanted to try and find the rock pool you showed him yesterday but he slipped and he cut his hand on a broken bottle hidden in the sand. I can't believe it happened. The beach is usually so clean.'

Luke bent down and looked Reuben in the eyes. 'Okay, big boy. I'm going to spray some magic stuff on here to make this nice and numb. Then I'll be able to clean it.'

The tears still rolled freely down Reuben's face and he sniffed loudly. 'I want my mommy.'

'I know, Reuben, but she will be here in a minute. Let me see if I can make this better.'

He gave the laceration a quick spray and waited

a few minutes before touching it. The cut was deeper than he'd first thought and would definitely need sutures. 'Can you give your fingers a wiggle for me, please, Reuben?'

'I want my mommy.'

'She's just coming, I promise. Now, let me see you wiggling your fingers.'

Reuben stuck out his bottom lip, before wiggling his fingers. Luke checked carefully, ensuring there was no further damage. He gave Lucy a rueful smile. 'There's no permanent damage,' he said, 'but I'm going to have to suture this.'

'You're going to have to what?' Abby had appeared in the doorway, white-faced and breathless. She crossed the room in two strides, wrapping her arms around Reuben and brushing against Luke's gloves in the process.

He stepped back to give her a few minutes.

'What happened, Lucy?'

'I'm really sorry, Abby, but he cut himself on the beach. Luke said that he needs some stitches.'

Luke was back over at the sink, throwing one set of gloves in the disposal bin and scrubbing his hands again. As he pulled on a fresh set of gloves, his eyes were drawn elsewhere. One of

Reuben's trousers legs had bunched up and revealed a dark purple bruise on the soft tissue at the
back of his shin. Had that been there last night?
He didn't think so. Or had it happened yesterday
when they'd been surfing? One thing he knew for
sure—a child shouldn't bruise that easily.

He gave Abby a quick smile. 'Are you okay with
me doing this, or do you want to get someone
else?' He was more than capable of suturing the
laceration but if Abby would prefer one of her
other colleagues, that was fine.

Abby shook her head. 'Sorry about the gloves,'
she murmured. 'I should know better.'

'No worries. You've got your mommy head on
right now. Do you want me to do the sutures?'

'Yes, please. As long as you don't mind his over-
anxious mother hanging over your shoulder.'

Luke smiled. 'No problems. But I should warn
you, I expect some singing while I'm doing this.'
He raised his eyebrows at Lucy, who quickly realised he wanted something to distract Reuben.

'We can do that, can't we, Abby?' She started
to sing a nursery rhyme.

Abby quickly joined in as Luke bent his head

and expertly inserted a row of sutures along the laceration then covered it with a white dressing.

'All done. Well done, Reuben.' He ruffled Reuben's hair with his hand. 'I think that deserves a special treat. How about I give Lucy some money to buy you a huge pancake at the canteen with chocolate syrup?'

Reuben's eyes widened like saucers, his injury quickly forgotten. 'Can I, Mommy? Please?'

Abby smiled. She didn't often indulge his sweet tooth, but her heart had stopped when her page had gone off, saying Reuben was in the ER. She was so relieved it was nothing serious.

'Of course you can, honey,' she said. 'I'll need to fill out a little paperwork at the front desk. I'll be there in a minute.'

Lucy picked up Reuben from the bed and headed towards the door with him. Luke caught Abby's arm as she headed towards the door.

'Abby…'

She noticed the expression on his face. 'What's wrong, Luke?'

'Maybe nothing. It's just, I noticed a new bruise at the back of Reuben's shin. Maybe it was there yesterday, but I don't remember it.'

Her face paled. A whirlwind of possibilities started flooding her mind. The last thing that the mother of a child with ALL wanted to hear. New bruises.

'But I watch him so carefully. I mean, I check all the time, I hadn't noticed anything...' Her voice drifted off.

A chill spread across her skin. She hadn't checked him carefully that morning. Not like she usually did. This morning her head had been filled with hot and steamy memories of the night before. Had she missed the bruise?

Luke slipped an arm around her waist. 'It might be nothing, Abby, I wasn't trying to alarm you. It's just...it caught my eye when I was stitching his hand, so I thought I better mention it.' Her weight had sagged against him and he could see the distress on her face as her mind raced to its own conclusions. He walked over to the reception desk with her. 'Look, you fill out the paperwork and I'll meet you in the canteen with Reuben, okay?'

She gave a little nod, her mind obviously distracted, and he bent over and lightly kissed her cheek. Her fingers lifted to her cheek and her eyes flickered over to meet his. 'What? Yes, okay. I'll see you in minute.'

Luke left her at the desk and strode through to the canteen, where Reuben was busy asking Jan to make him the biggest pancake possible. He lifted Reuben from Lucy's arms. 'Will you go and see that Abby's all right?' he asked, and she nodded silently and headed back towards the door.

'One extra-large pancake with chocolate sauce.' Jan placed the plate on a tray next to a glass of milk. She glanced at Luke's full arms. 'Do you want me to carry this over to one of the tables?'

He gave a quick nod and walked behind her to a table looking out over the gardens.

'I get the window seat!' shouted Reuben, and wriggled out of Luke's arms, plunking himself down in the seat next to the glass. 'Yum, yum!' He licked his lips in anticipation as the plate was pushed in front of him. 'Can you help me cut it up, Dr Luke?' he asked as he held out a knife.

Luke smiled and started cutting the pancake into manageable chunks. His mind was whirring with the possibilities of ALL. Had he seen something minor and jumped to a dramatic conclusion? His instincts said no.

'My mommy's the best cutter,' murmured Reuben as he watched Luke's efforts. 'She cuts in triangles, they're much easier to get in my mouth.'

'Does she now?' said Luke with amusement, as he tried to re-jig his efforts into triangular pieces. 'How's that?'

'Mmm, it'll do.' Reuben lifted his fork and speared a piece of pancake, the chocolate sauce inevitably dripping down the front of his T-shirt.

Luke felt as if he was holding his breath. The more time he spent in this little boy's company, the more familiar he felt. It wasn't just the eyes and hair colour. It was his mannerisms. The things that he did without even realising it. The way he played with a little tuft of hair on his forehead, just as Ryan had. The way that his pinkie nail, *and only his pinkie nail*, on both hands was bitten down to the quick. The same way his own had always been as a child.

'Whatya looking at, Dr Luke? Do ya want a piece of my pancake?' Reuben was brandishing his fork, dripping with chocolate sauce towards Luke.

'No, thanks, Reuben. You eat it all.'

Luke bit his bottom lip. Ryan had died of ALL

and this little boy had ALL too. Four years old compared to Ryan's fifteen. Life was so unfair sometimes. Children didn't deserve a disease like this. Children didn't deserve to suffer. Why did this little boy—Abby's little boy—have to have ALL?

Luke raised his eyes skyward. Was somebody up there trying to send him a message? There was nothing in the world that Luke wanted more than the chance to have his brother back. The same wild wish or dream shared by every family the world over who had ever lost a loved one.

Maybe he could get a chance to do all the things with Reuben that he never could with Ryan?

But as much as he cared about Abby, could he really do this? Losing Ryan had been the single most painful experience of his life. He'd seen first-hand the devastation the disease caused. He would be mad to put himself through that again.

The swing door for the canteen opened and a still pale-faced Abby crossed the room with a weak smile on her face. She slid into the chair next to Reuben, giving him a kiss on top of his head.

'Look, Mommy,' he said, swirling a piece of

pancake in the remaining chocolate sauce. 'This is great.'

She slipped an arm around his shoulders. 'I'm sure it is, honey.' Her eyes met Luke's, and she looked as if she were in pain. 'I'm going to take the rest of the day off and go home with Reuben,' she said quietly.

'Do you want some company?'

She shook her head. 'No. I need for us to have a little time together. Just the two of us.'

Luke nodded. It wasn't the first time he'd heard her talk like this. Right from the start she'd said that Reuben was hers and hers alone. She didn't seem to have made room in her life for anyone else. It was almost as if she didn't want to share Reuben, and wanted to keep him all to herself.

But she shouldn't have to shoulder the burden alone. He could see the haunted look on her face. He could almost reach out and touch the physical pain she was feeling. It was evident in every little line on her forehead and around her strained eyes.

Right now, for Abby's sake, he had to try and make the effort. He had to offer her the support she so clearly needed—and that he'd never had.

No one should have to do this on their own. And it didn't matter how mixed up he felt.

She'd looked distinctly uncomfortable that morning, when she'd found Reuben playing on top of Luke's bed. Something churned deep down in his stomach. Luke stood up and straightened his coat, walking around to Reuben's seat. 'Yuck! Look at those chocolate hands. What do you say that I take you to clean up a little while your mom gets changed out of her scrubs?' He gave Abby a little nod as he bent to pick up Reuben. 'See you in five minutes, okay?'

He held Reuben's hands under the faucet. He could manage this. The simple stuff. The hand-washing and toy-soldier-playing stuff.

'Why is Mommy sad?' The innocent question almost stopped Luke dead. Children were so perceptive.

'Do you think Mommy is sad?'

Reuben nodded. 'She has the sad face on today.'

Luke knelt on the floor to face him. 'Sometimes adults are a little sad. It doesn't mean that you've done anything to make her sad, though.'

'I know.' He leaned forward and whispered in Luke's ear, 'When Mommy's sad, I get to sleep in the big bed with her. My cuddles make her all better.'

Luke smiled. 'Well, they sound like really special cuddles. I'm sure they do make Mommy feel better.' He took a deep breath and swept up Reuben into his arms. What he wouldn't give right now to cuddle Abby in the big bed. But if he wanted to find a way into Abby's heart, he was going to have to let Reuben into his.

CHAPTER NINE

ABBY could feel the bile rise in the back of her throat. Her stomach was churning and she felt physically sick. *Please don't let there be anything wrong with my little boy.* She sent her prayer upward as she finished signing a form at the desk.

'Hi, Mommy!'

Her human cannonball sped across the department and wrapped his arms around her legs. She could feel the prickle of tears in her eyes.

'I just got the best swing from Dr Luke.'

From Luke? Really?

Luke walked in slowly behind Reuben, touching her arm as he approached her at the desk. 'Are you going home?'

His voice was quiet, steady. He knew exactly where her priorities lay and he was letting her know that he understood. For once, it was a relief to have someone around who knew exactly how she felt. Who didn't prod or pry. Or ask a million questions. He didn't have to—because he'd *been* here.

She gave a little nod and bent to pick up Reuben, trying hard not to let her gaze fixate on his legs.

'Are you going to be okay?' Luke's concern almost made the hair on her arms stand on end. That reassurance. Having someone there to support you. She'd never had that before with Reuben. Last time around she'd dealt with everything herself. How easy it would be to have someone to lean on.

She gave him a smile. 'We'll be fine.' Her voice caught, she hesitated. 'You'll be home for dinner, won't you?'

His breath caught in his throat. *Home for dinner.* It sounded like something else entirely. It sounded almost like a ready-made life. Something that right now he would kill for. For the first time ever he felt as if they were in the same place. He'd heard the hesitation as she'd said those words. She meant exactly the same thing he did. Home. He ruffled Reuben's hair. 'Of course I will. Do you want me to bring something in?'

Abby shook her head. 'Oh, no. Reuben and I have that covered. We're going to make something special.' She bent her head, whispering in Reuben's ear, 'Aren't we, honey?'

Reuben's eyes gleamed conspiratorially. 'Oh, yes.' He nodded. 'You'll like it, Dr Luke.'

'I'm sure I will.'

He watched Abby leave the department and walk along the coastal path, Reuben still safely held in her arms. As if she didn't want to let him go. A slow feeling of dread crept through him. And it had filled his heart in a way he'd never thought possible. A way he'd never dared to feel.

This was about him. This was all about him. It was the first moment ever he'd actually taken some time to consider what his infertility meant to him. Not to Abby, or anyone else, but to *him*. He'd never admitted to anyone how much he wanted a family. He'd never admitted to *himself* that he might want a family. And until it was right under his nose, he'd never really known how *much* he wanted a family. And now he did. And it terrified him.

Abby was right. Families came in all shapes and sizes. And all with a possibility of heart-break. Reuben had ALL. And he had already lived through that experience. Reuben could die.

If he opened his heart to this little boy, he might have to live through all this again. Could he really do that? Could he really put himself out there to endure that physical, psychological, crushing pain all over again?

But what was more important? The chance to experience the love and joy of a family—no matter what pain came with it? Or the bury-your-head-in-your-career option? Where he pretended it was never what he'd wanted in the first place.

But now there was something much more important at stake. This wasn't just about him. He already felt a connection to Abby and Reuben that he could never have imagined. He couldn't have seen more pain in Abby's face if he'd ripped her heart out with a spoon. Biological child or not, she was Reuben's mother. In every way that mattered.

But where did that leave him?

Abby resisted the temptation to run along the path at top speed, get Reuben home and strip his clothes off in a flash. He was very perceptive to her mood and she didn't want to do anything to alarm him. Anything to let him think he was sick again.

Reuben cuddled into her chest as the wind

picked up. Was he tired? Was it another symptom that she'd missed?

He was so light in her arms. Had he lost weight?

As they approached the house his blond head picked up. 'Let me down, Mommy, I want a shot on the slide.'

He wriggled free from her arms and ran off towards the slide, climbing the steps at a rate of knots and slipping down the slide. 'Wheeeee...'

He wasn't tired. He had as much energy as ever. She reached for his hand as he slid down for a second time. 'Let's go in and get changed, Reuben.'

He stared down at his jogging trousers and T-shirt. 'What's wrong with these?'

She pointed to a few chocolate stains and an earlier smattering of blood. 'They're all dirty. Lets get some nice clean clothes on.'

'I'll choose, I'll choose,' he shouted as he mounted the steps at the front of the house.

Abby turned the lock on the front door. 'Race you upstairs,' she said, as she dumped her bag in the corridor and watched him disappear ahead of her. By the time she reached Reuben's room, he'd already pulled a rainbow's worth of T-shirts from one of his drawers. 'Red—no, yellow—no, green,' he said at the array of clothing at his feet.

Her heart was pounding in her chest. She knelt down before him. 'Okay, pumpkin, lift your arms.'

Reuben automatically raised his hands above his head as she pulled the T-shirt up. She was holding her breath as her eyes swept over his torso. 'Turn around, honey,' she instructed, and he dutifully spun round. Nothing. There was nothing there. No bruises. No blotches. Nothing to worry her. She felt the air leave her lungs.

'Let's take these dirty trousers off too.' She pulled at the elastic waistband on the joggers, sliding them downwards, and drew in her breath sharply.

Three. There were three angry purple bruises that hadn't been there that morning. Bruises that, if she'd seen them on any other child, she would have thought were a few days old.

Reuben's eyes followed hers. 'Wow! Look, Mommy, where did they come from?' He dropped to the floor, his spread-out legs filling him with wonder. He prodded at the purple bruises. 'They don't hurt.'

Abby caught his hand. 'Don't do that, honey.'

She pulled him over into her arms for a cuddle. Her hand automatically went to his head and stroked his hair in a soothing motion. 'Mommy's going to have to put some magic cream on your arms again.'

Reuben wrinkled his nose. 'Not blood tests,' he groaned. His childlike brain was filling in the gaps. He shook his head determinedly. 'I don't need any.'

'I'm sorry, honey. But Mommy has to take some blood to make sure you're okay.'

'No.' He stamped his foot on the floor.

It broke her heart. Reuben had already spent too many of his young hours in hospitals. The last thing she wanted to do was make him go back. But her paediatric head was screaming at her. This could be the first sign he was out of remission. She tried to take a step back and look at him through professional eyes.

He wasn't breathless. He had a good appetite. He hadn't complained of any bone or joint pains. She ran her hands over his body, looking for lumps in the neck, underarms or groin. Nothing.

But he was pale. But Reuben was always pale. Was he paler than normal?

'Let's get some clean clothes on.' She picked up one of the T-shirts from the floor. 'Now, which colour? Red or blue?'

'Blue,' he shouted, and she pulled it quickly over his head. Her hands hesitated over the drawer, nearly pulling out a pair of shorts, before stopping and finding another pair of joggers instead. She couldn't bear the thought of staring at those purple bruises all evening and what they might mean.

'Mommy needs to make a phone call, honey. Let's go down to the kitchen and get a snack. Do you want to watch some cartoons?' Anything to keep him occupied while she phoned the paediatric oncologist. She already knew what he'd say. He'd want blood tests and a bone-marrow aspiration. A procedure that Reuben hated.

Blood tests she could do. The bone-marrow aspiration would have to be done elsewhere. She'd have to arrange a few days off.

Abby continued on autopilot for the rest of the day. It was almost a relief when Luke walked through the door at six o'clock, because it gave her an excuse to focus on something else.

'Hi, Luke, dinner is just about ready. Go and wash up.'

Luke took in the forced happiness and smile that seemed to be pasted on her face. All he could see was the stress she was putting herself under.

He hung his jacket on the coat stand behind the door and crossed over to the kitchen window next to her. With no attempt to hide his intentions, his arms caught her in a hug as he dropped a kiss on her head. 'How are you?'

He caught the shiver that ran down her spine. Her voice was tight. 'Just what you'd expect. I've drawn the bloods and spoken to the oncologist. I'll take him to San Francisco on Thursday for his bone marrow.'

Thursday, two days away. Probably the quickest they could arrange it.

'Have you told him?'

'No.' Her voice cracked. 'But he's not stupid. He's been through all this before. Sometimes he seems so much older than four.' Her voice drifted off as she gazed out the window. 'But, then again, he's been through much more than the average four-year-old.'

Luke moved away from the worktop, sitting down on the comfortable easy chair that faced onto the garden and pulling her onto his lap. 'And how are *you*, Abby?' he asked again.

'I'll be fine.' Her face was still fixed towards the garden. It was apparent to him that she couldn't look at him.

'You don't need to go through this on your own. I'm right here.' His voice was deep, rich and reassuring.

'But you're not here, Luke.' Her head whipped around towards him, two pink spots appearing on her cheeks. 'This is just a coincidence. In another two days you'll be flying off to your jet-set lifestyle in DC. And I'll be taking my little boy for a test that he absolutely hates.'

She was angry. She was angry that he was trying to comfort her, trying to help. He wasn't helping. He was confusing things for her. She needed to focus on Reuben. She needed to focus on her son.

Luke took a deep breath. The Abby Tyler he'd known had always coped with everything. Nothing had fazed her. But the Abby Tyler he'd known hadn't had a child with ALL. A child who could come out of remission at any point.

He took her hand in his. 'I'm here now, Abby. Why don't we just focus on that? Stop imagining what could happen, because the doctor in you will always consider the worst-case scenario. These last two days have been the most…' his eyes lifted upwards as he searched for the word '…*interesting* I've had in the last five years.' His other hand lifted to her face, pushing a wayward blonde lock back behind her ear so he could see the whole of her face. The whole of her.

'Our timing really sucks. But maybe you're not the only one who needed to re-evaluate their life. Maybe seeing you here, like this, has been just the kick up the butt that I needed.'

He glanced into the living room, where Reuben was sitting on the bright rug in front of the television, watching cartoons to his heart's content. 'He is the luckiest little boy in the world, and that's because he's got you.'

'But what happens if I'm not enough? What happens if I can't be strong enough for him?' Her voice was trembling and one large tear trickled down her cheek and dripped from her chin.

'You will be, Abby, and you are. You always will be.'

He stood up and walked towards the old range cooker. He could have said something completely different there. But he had to be sure about how he felt. He had to know if he could do this all over again. Maybe in a few days…

'What this?' He bent over the large crock-pot, lifting the lid and pulling back at the escaping steam.

Abby rubbed her eyes, conscious of the obvious subject change. 'It's our "something special". Reuben adds everything he likes from the fridge and the pantry.' She leaned over and gave it a stir with a wooden spoon before shrugging her shoulders. 'Usually it's not too bad—some chicken, potatoes, carrot, turnip and some kind of stock. But today Reuben decided his magic ingredient was a can of baked beans.' She gave a little shiver. 'Needless to say, you'll be getting the biggest portion.'

Luke leaned back against the worktop, a grimace on his face. 'I'm sure it'll be delicious.' He wrinkled his nose. 'What else can I smell?' He bent downwards and peered through the oven door. 'What's that?'

'Marshmallow and chocolate loaf.'

He raised his eyebrow at her. 'That sounds healthy.'

She snapped her tea towel at him. 'Shut up. It's comfort food for me. I need it.'

Luke gave a little nod and folded his arms across his chest. 'I know someone else who could use a little comfort food.'

'Who?'

'Jennifer Taylor. She's climbing the walls in there.' He nodded his head up towards the hospital. 'She asked if you would drop in and see her later.' His voice dropped slightly, 'Obviously I never told her anything about Reuben.'

Abby's head turned towards the living room where Reuben was sitting. 'But I can't. I need to—'

He placed his hand on her shoulder. 'You need to take a break and go eat your comfort food with someone else. I'll watch Reuben. Why don't you go along after dinner and take your mind off things?'

She shot him a look of exasperation.

'I know, I know, but a change of scene might do you some good.'

A loud, belly laugh came from next door. Something in the cartoon had caught Reuben's imagination and filled the house with little-boy laughter.

The sound twisted in her gut, bringing yet another tear to her eye. How much longer would she be able to hear it? Maybe Luke was right. Maybe she did need a break—even if it was only for half an hour.

She sighed. 'Are you sure you don't mind?' She looked towards the front door. 'A walk along the path might clear my head a little. And it might be nice to offer Jennifer some support. I don't suppose James Turner is a bundle of laughs.'

It only took her five minutes to wander back along the coastal path to the hospital. She could probably have been quicker if she hadn't stopped to pick some flowers from her garden for Jennifer.

The hospital seemed pretty quiet, with only the black sporadically placed mumbling men giving any hint that anything out the ordinary was happening.

The man at the door gave her a little nod and moved to the side as she entered. Jennifer was lying on her side, watching television, still attached to the drip and looking bored to tears.

'Abby!' she said, sitting up in bed and reaching for the remote control.

'Hi, Jennifer. Luke said you were a little bored, so I thought I'd come and see you.' Abby sat down on the bed beside her and glanced at the pile of books and DVDs on the bedside table. 'How many of these have you read?'

Jennifer gave a guilty smile, as if she were a teenager caught out misbehaving. 'I've watched all the DVDs but don't take them away—I'll watch them again. And I've only got one book left to read. I'm a sucker for romance novels.'

Abby ran her eyes up the pile of books then looked at her in amazement. 'You've read all those books already?'

Jennifer shrugged. 'Reading is my passion. I just never normally get the time to do it.' She shuffled some of the books out of the way to make room for Abby's package. 'What's this?' She inhaled deeply, catching the whiff of melted chocolate and marshmallows. 'It smells gorgeous.' She unwrapped the tea towel surrounding it, letting the aroma fill the room. 'Whoa!'

Abby gave her a little smile. 'Comfort food. Thought you might want to eat it with me.' She lifted the bunch of flowers in her hand. 'I brought you some flowers too, but I see that everyone else had the same idea.'

Every available space in the room was filled with exuberant displays of multicoloured flowers. Jennifer waved her hand at them. 'They look gorgeous, but most of them have no perfume.' She took the bunch from Abby's hand. 'Now, these...' she inhaled '...smell wonderful.' She lay back against her pillows, a tiny little crease forming across her forehead. 'So what do you need comfort food for, Abby Tyler?'

Abby bit her bottom lip and rolled her eyes. She couldn't possibly tell her the real reason. She couldn't even get her head around the thought that Reuben might be unwell again, so the last thing she wanted to do was speculate. Not when there was another, easier answer she could give Jennifer. She gave her a little smile. 'It's not easy, living under the same roof as your ex again.'

A gleam appeared in Jennifer's eyes. 'Oh, do tell. This place has been mind-numbingly boring today.'

Abby unpacked a blunt knife and started cutting the marshmallow and chocolate loaf. She pointed to Jennifer's belly. 'You tell first. Any sign of Junior making an appearance yet?'

Jennifer swung her legs off the bed and switched on a latte machine in the corner of the room. She laughed at Abby's raised eyebrows. 'It's the only perk I've got, okay?' She gave her hip a little rub. 'Nothing's happening at all. Nothing. *Nada*. They gave me some steroids today to help mature Junior's lungs.' She pointed a finger at Abby. 'And you're in *big* trouble, Dr Tyler, for not telling me how much that would sting!'

Abby laughed. 'Oops, sorry, I might have forgotten to mention that.'

Jennifer shook her head in disgust. 'Sure you did. They gave me some more antibiotics as well.' She wrinkled her nose. 'And there's only been the tiniest trickle today, so I guess that must be good.' She pressed a few buttons on the machine as Abby put the loaf onto some plates.

A few seconds later Jennifer handed a steaming mug to her. 'Don't get too excited. It's a caffeine-free latte.' A smile crept across her face as she eyed the gooey melted marshmallows and chocolate. 'Now, this is what I call *comfort food*.' She took a big bite. 'Yum.'

Abby nodded as she took a sip of the coffee. 'I agree. So what can I do to liven this place up for you?' She nodded at all the flowers. 'Does anyone know that you're here? I haven't seen any reporters or television crews about.'

'No, no. They're just from my husband and his few "closest" aides. Hopefully we'll get this baby safely out before the newshounds get wind of it.' She settled back against her pillows again. 'What's the story with Lincoln Adams? He's a friend of yours, isn't he?'

'Yes, he is.' The oozing, warm marshmallow melted in her mouth. Yup. Luke had been right, this was definitely making her feel better.

'How come a man as handsome as that looks so incredibly sad? Have I dragged him away from his wife and children? Is he unhappy about looking after me?' Her brow was furrowed.

Abby shrugged her shoulders. 'To be honest, Linc hasn't said much since he's been here. But his mood…it's been like that for a while. I'm not sure what's going on with him.' And she hadn't asked him either. What with the First Lady being in her hospital, her ex appearing and now Reuben's bruising, she hadn't even thought to ask Linc what was

222 THE BOY WHO MADE THEM LOVE AGAIN

wrong. Some friend she was. Maybe it was time she sat him down for a chat? She made a mental note to do that and changed the subject rapidly, 'What do you think of David Fairgreaves?'

Jennifer broke into a big smile. 'Oh, I love him! He's just like a grumpy old man. You should *hear* the way he talks to James Turner. I don't think I've ever heard anyone be so indifferent towards him. Sometimes he just completely ignores him.' She took another bite from her loaf. 'You know what? I'm going to pack him up in a big box and take him back to Washington with me.'

'It's going to have to be a pretty big box.'

'How come?'

'He doesn't go anywhere without that fishing boat.'

The door was pushed open and James Turner stuck his head inside, to be met by instant laughter from the two women. 'Just checking on you, Mrs Taylor.' He caught sight of the sticky mess on the plates and rolled his eyes at Abby. 'But I see that Dr Bad Influence has already got things under control.'

'She certainly has, Mr Turner.' Jennifer licked her fingers. 'Best medicine I've had since I got here, Abby.' She glanced over to the windows, her gaze settling on the ocean view. 'You know, Pelican Cove's not too shabby. I get so swept up in living in a big city that I forget about the small-town stuff. I think this has done me the world of good.'

'How so?'

She dropped her hands down on the bed. 'Well, it's certainly been *restful*.' She rolled her eyes at Abby. 'I probably wasn't resting the way I should have been.' Her hands lay on top of her stomach. 'Now, seriously, I need to ask you something.'

Abby lifted her head. 'What is it?'

Jennifer's brow wrinkled. 'Well, actually, David Fairgreaves told me to speak to you. I asked him about umbilical stem cells. He told me a little but he said to ask you. How come? I thought he was the world-renowned expert on it all.'

Abby gave a slow smile. 'He is. But it's his "baby". He knows so much about it all he tends to get all technical when he talks about it. He wouldn't want to get carried away and blind you with science. Plus, he'd be worried that you wouldn't consider him to be impartial. And because he's so enthusiastic about the subject, it's easy to see why. Were you thinking about collecting the cells?'

'To be honest, I wasn't sure. But if there was a possibility it could be useful in the future…'

Abby sat on the side of her bed. 'You do realise it isn't always successful? Sometimes they can't extract enough cells from the cord.'

'What do you think? And why did he tell me to talk to you?'

Abby looked at her sadly. 'As a physician I think it is a good idea. It's not going to do you or your baby any harm, in some areas the cord would be thrown away, but the possibilities for the future could be great.' Her head turned towards the window. 'I told you things were complicated.' She ran her fingers through her hair. 'My son has leukaemia. One of the types of cancer that can be treated with stem cells. So I guess I'm not entirely impartial either, I'm a bit biased about the possibilities.'

Jennifer's hand flew to her mouth. 'Reuben has leukaemia? Oh, Abby, I'm so sorry.'

The tears formed in her eyes again. Abby took a deep breath. 'We don't really know all the possibilities for stem cells as yet. They can treat some kinds of cancer, some autoimmune disorders, there's research into Alzheimer's, diabetes, Parkinson's disease. But it seems that we learn something new every day. There are still risks, certain genetic conditions can be contained in the stem cells. But, on the other hand, it might be the best insurance policy your child could have.' She gave Jennifer's hand a squeeze. 'You need to consider all the possibilities. And you need to decide if this is the right decision for you. I'll print out some information that you can read in your own time. If you decide to go for it, the hospital would usually receive a collection kit from whichever company you've decided to use. If the collection is successful, they normally have a courier collect it and take it to their storage facility.'

Jennifer nodded thoughtfully. 'I'll talk to Charlie about it later. Thank you for tonight, Abby. It's great to have some company. And I'm sorry about Reuben. Is he going to be okay?'

Abby bit her bottom lip. 'I'm not sure. He needs to have some tests done again. But I'm hopeful.'

'Then so am I.' She leaned back against the pillows. 'I think you're really lucky, staying here.'

Abby raised her eyebrow. 'In comparison to the

city? I took you for a city girl, Jennifer Taylor—not a country bumpkin like me.'

'But it's different here. What I like most about this place is the people, the sense of community. You lose all that in the big cities. Here…' she gestured outwards '…everyone knows everyone. The guy that is the janitor, Davie, his wife works in the kitchen and his daughter works at the local school. The nurse who looked after me this morning has three generations of her family all living in Pelican Cove. The girl who does the cleaning, her little brother goes to the local Special ed school. I like that.' She turned and faced Abby. 'This must be a great place to bring up a little boy.'

Reuben. Tears pricked her eyes again. She was a mess. Was she going to burst into tears every time she thought about him? She had to get a hold of herself.

She gave Jennifer a little smile. 'It is a great place to bring up a child. Particularly if, like me, you don't have any family. That's why I moved here. I holidayed here as a child and there is a real sense of community spirit here. The people here embrace you, and draw you into their community.

That's what I want for my little boy. A real sense of family.'

'And can't you get that with someone else?' The words were heavily weighted.

Abby took a deep breath. 'Not everyone wants a family, not everyone's that good with kids,' she said quietly.

Jennifer reached over and took her hand. 'I don't know if Charlie or I are going to be that good with kids, Abby. But in a few days' time we'll find out. And hopefully we'll learn as we go. Things aren't always what they seem. Luke was in here earlier, talking about you and Reuben. His face comes alive when he talks about you both. Don't tell me that doesn't mean something.'

She shook her head. 'Luke doesn't want a family.'

'No. Five years ago, he *didn't* want a family. Have you asked him what he wants now?'

'I don't know how appropriate it is to have that conversation. It's been five years. I'm living a completely different life now. One that I don't know if Luke would like.'

'No. That's not it.' Jennifer folded her arms across her chest.

'What do you mean?'

'This isn't about what Luke wants. This is about what *you* want.'

'I don't understand. What do you mean?'

'Abby, I'm a lawyer. I've spent fifteen years reading between the lines, hearing the things that people haven't actually said. You still find him attractive, don't you?'

Abby could feel the colour flooding her cheeks. 'Obviously.'

'Then this has to be about Reuben. Is there a problem with his father?'

Abby shifted uncomfortably in her seat. 'There is no father. Reuben's adopted. It's complicated.'

'Abby, life is complicated. Ah. I get it.' Jennifer leaned back, nodding her head thoughtfully.

'Get what?' Abby was bewildered. She had no idea what was going on in this conversation. She just knew that little bells and whistles were currently going off in her brain.

'You don't want to share.'

'What?' Abby was stunned.

'Reuben. You don't want to share Reuben.'

'But—'

'But nothing. Reuben is all yours. You've built

a comfortable life here for you both. And you're worried about how Luke could upset all that. You're also worried about being replaced in Reuben's affections. It's obvious they're naturally drawn to one another. You don't want to share.'

'That's a ridiculous thing to say.' Abby stood up, lifting the plates and walking over to the sink.

'If it's a ridiculous thing to say, why do you feel so uncomfortable?'

Abby sloshed warm water on the plates, scrubbing them furiously. She didn't have an answer.

Jennifer rested her arms on her distended stomach. 'That's the great thing about kids, Abby—or so I hear. They give lots of unconditional love. And once you've experienced it, I imagine it's a pretty hard thing to share.'

Abby finished washing the plates and grabbed some paper towels to dry them. She sat them at the side of the sink and turned around to face Jennifer, folding her arms across her chest in self-preservation mode.

Her voice was low and steady. 'People must run a mile when they see you enter a courtroom.'

Jennifer nodded. 'Yup. They usually do.'

'Next time I need a lawyer, you'd better be available.'

'I'm always available for friends.'

There was silence for a few seconds. Abby contemplating the words that Jennifer had just said to her. Little pieces were making sense. The way she'd felt when she'd seen them spending time at the beach together yesterday—something that he'd always done with her. Could she share?

Abby wandered back along the coastal path, admiring the beauty of her surroundings. The sun was setting over the horizon, sending orange and red streams of colour across the ocean. The smell of the sea air and the brightly coloured flowers littering the coastal path made her realise that it wasn't just the community here that made her happy. It was the whole place, the whole environment, the best possible place for she and Reuben to be. But was this somewhere Luke would want to be?

It was an uncomfortable thought because she knew what the answer to that question was. Pelican Cove wasn't a place for someone who was building their career and wanted to be at the top of their field. Pelican Cove wasn't the place new research was carried out and new discoveries were made. Pelican Cove was a place where life ticked along happily, and there was time for people and families.

Abby couldn't live in a city again. Her priorities had changed. This was the life she wanted. And there wasn't a place for Luke here.

She stopped at her white picket fence and looked in towards her house. She could see through her front bay window right inside her living room. Luke was sitting on the floor with Reuben in front of the dimly flickering fire. Reuben was animated, running circles around Luke and talking nineteen to the dozen, and for the first time Luke didn't look distinctly uncomfortable. He was obviously trying to make an effort—but how did that make him feel?

How did that make *her* feel?

Reuben had never really had a father figure in his life. Sure, he'd played with some of Abby's male colleagues, but most of the time it was just her and him. She hadn't really given much thought to what he might be missing out on.

Something twisted inside her. Was this her fault?

She'd always imagined that she was giving her son everything that he needed. But what if he needed more than her?

The window banged. Reuben and Luke had spotted her at the garden gate and were gesturing for her to come inside and join the battle. She gave a little wave and started up the path.

Reuben met her at the door. 'I'm winning, Mommy,' he shouted as he sent a sponge ball flying across the living room.

'I can see that.'

Luke crossed the room and slipped an arm around her waist. 'Is everything okay? How did you get on with Jennifer?'

'We got on fine. Has Reuben been good?'

She watched as he sent a toy truck careering into a legion of soldiers, catapulting them around the room.

'Yes, Reuben's been fine. Can I do anything for you?'

Abby leaned her head against his shoulder. Comfort was nice. Relying on someone was nice. Having some you trusted look after your child, someone that wasn't just a childcare worker, was reassuring. Someone that felt like family. She slipped one arm around his back and put the other on his chest. The heat radiated through her, filling her with warmth and compassion that was more than just a comfort.

She lifted her head and gave him a smile. 'Yes, you can.' Her fingers played with the button on his shirt. 'I want you to hold me, just like this, all night.'

Luke nodded. She needed him. For the first time in her life Abby really needed him. He kissed her on the forehead. 'Your wish is my command,' he whispered as they watched Reuben play.

CHAPTER TEN

Abby's eyes flickered over to the white board. There were currently fourteen patients in the ER, six of whom were children. It was busier than normal, with patients appearing to crawl out of the woodwork on the dull, overcast day.

Her eyes caught the tail of Luke's white coat as he swept into the trauma room to deal with the third chest pain of the day. What were they going to do in a few days' time when he went back to Washington? They hadn't managed to arrange a replacement yet for Valerie Carter, their cardiologist, who'd just delivered a bouncing baby boy.

There was a little nudge at her elbow. David Fairgreaves, for once dressed immaculately in theatre scrubs, gave her a little smile. 'It's day four and Jennifer Taylor's just started to labour. I'll let you know when we've got a baby.' He gave her a little wink and disappeared around the corner. A shiver ran down Abby's spine. Pelican Cove would well and truly be on the map once the First Son or Daughter arrived. Did this mean the President would be coming? James Turner would spontaneously combust!

For the next few hours she worked steadily, seeing one child after another. Asthma attacks, nettle stings, tiny things stuck in places they should never be made the time fly past. By lunchtime she was ready for a break, but there was still one child to be seen. She lifted the chart and trudged behind the curtains. A familiar face sat in front of her. Jon King was a teenage skateboarder and spent his spare time in her emergency room, getting the latest part of his body stitched back up again. She gave a sigh. 'What is it this time, Jon?'

He lifted his elbow, which had a large blood-soaked dressing pad on it. She gave a nod of her head. 'Right, let's get this cleaned up and see what we can do.'

Ten minutes later, Lincoln Adams stuck his head around the curtains.

'Abby, can I steal you for a while?' A wicked smile spread across his lips. 'It's a special request.'

Abby looked up as she finished snipping her last stitch. 'There you are, good as new, Jon.' The teenager gave her a nod as he examined his latest row of sutures in his elbow. 'Nancy will put a dressing over that.'

She snapped off her gloves and rinsed her hands at the sink before joining Linc outside the curtain. 'What's up?'

He wrinkled his nose. 'Things are progressing quicker than expected and I'd like another pair of hands in the room.' He paused for a second. 'And right now I strongly suspect Jennifer Taylor could do with the moral support.'

'Doesn't she have anyone with her?'

He shook his head. 'Her husband isn't here yet and she's thrown all her aides out of the room. It's medical personnel only.'

Abby gave a nod. 'If you need me, I'm yours.'

'Fabulous. Come on.'

He led her down the corridor and they pushed past the six men in black positioned outside the door. 'I think we're going to need Luke,' mumbled Abby. 'James Turner looks as if he could have a heart attack.'

Linc shot her a smile and nodded in the direction of the corner of the room where Dr Blair, the original obstetrician, sat positioned in a chair.

'We might need Luke anyway. It seems that the family obstetrician doesn't want to miss the main event—cardiac condition or not.'

'Abby, you're here. Thank you.'

Jennifer's voice sounded strained. Her face was pale and sweating, with strands of hair sticking to her forehead.

Abby walked over and picked up the nearby hairbrush from the locker and automatically started combing Jennifer's hair from her eyes, re-doing her hair and pulling it into a ponytail, just like she would have wanted someone to do for her. 'Can I give you a shoulder rub?' she asked as she positioned herself on the bed to support Jennifer.

Jennifer sighed and leaned back against her. 'That would be great, Abby.'

Abby lifted her hands and started kneading away the tight knots in Jennifer's shoulders. 'How are we doing, David?'

David gave her a relaxed smile. He looked like the cat who had got the cream. Not like a man who was about to deliver the premature First Baby.

'We're doing great.' He gave Jennifer's hand a squeeze. '*Mom* is doing great. Almost fully dilated and this baby will be crowning any time soon. The main man had better get a move on. This baby waits for nobody—President or not.'

Jennifer gave a little gasp as another contraction hit her. 'But I don't want to do this without Charlie. I need him here with me.'

Lincoln Adams took a look at her face. The last thing he needed right now was a stressed mom. 'I'll get an update,' he said as he stuck his head outside the door. There were muffled voices. 'Five minutes. James Turner is apparently out on the helicopter pad, waiting for him.'

Jennifer sagged back against Abby as the contraction eased. 'Thank the Lord,' she breathed, and turned her weary head towards Linc. 'Is this where I tell you I really, really want to push?'

He glanced towards David, who gave a nod of his head. 'We're ready when you are, Jennifer. On the next contraction feel free to push as hard as you like. I'll tell you when to stop.'

Jennifer glanced towards the window as the noise of a helicopter approaching grew louder. Seconds later the sounds of thudding feet came down the hall.

Abby held her breath as the door swung open and the President swept into the room. James

Turner and the rest of the security detail came to a halt at the door as it swung shut.

Jennifer gritted her teeth as another contraction racked her body. 'What time do you call this, Charlie Taylor?'

Abby bit her lip as the man she'd only ever seen on television before dodged around the multitude of bodies in the room. He only had eyes for his wife. Abby slid out from behind the First Lady to give him room and went to take her place by Lincoln at the neonate cot.

She watched as Charlie Taylor, the President of the United States, kissed his wife on the forehead and then gently on each tensed eyelid. 'I love you, baby,' he whispered. 'And there's nowhere else I'd rather bc.' He slid into place behind her, supporting her shoulders and sliding his arms around her stomach, feeling the contraction grip her. His eyes lifted, acknowledging the others in the room but resting on David. 'Everything okay?'

David smiled, as if he spoke to the President every day. 'Let's get this baby out.'

For Abby it was surreal. She stood in a room, surrounded by others but feeling as if she was the only person there. The slippery bundle was delivered within minutes, David lifting the baby out and laying her on top of her mom's stomach. Lincoln sprang into action, checking the baby while the cord was cut and clamped and Mom and Dad had a cuddle.

A minute later he carried the First Daughter over to the neonate cot for a full examination. Abby breathed a sigh of relief as he did the routine newborn checks. She could see for herself that the little girl was breathing and her colour was good. A few seconds later she let out a hearty cry. Lincoln finished his checks, wrapped her in a blanket and took her back over to her parents.

'Here we go,' he said, handing her over. 'A beautiful baby girl. 4 pounds 10 ounces—not bad for 32 weeks. She's breathing well and her colour is good, but we will need to monitor her for the next few days. We will need to keep a careful eye on her feeding too, but for now she's all yours.'

Jennifer breathed a huge sigh of relief as she and her husband bent over their baby daughter.

'Hi, gorgeous.' Charlie Taylor stroked his daughter's face. 'Just like your mommy.' He bent over and gave Jennifer a kiss.

David smiled. 'Do we have a name for the First Daughter, Mom and Dad?'

Jennifer looked up at her husband with tear-filled eyes. 'Well, do we, Charlie?'

The President gave a little smile. 'Jennifer got to pick the boy's name and I got to pick the girl's name. So our daughter will be called Esther Rose Taylor. After Jennifer's grandmother.' He gathered his wife and daughter in a warm embrace as the rest of the staff smiled and nodded at the gesture.

Esther, a biblical name. Just like Reuben's. But Abby hadn't got to choose Reuben's name. It had been the one he'd come with and she would have never dreamed of changing it.

Abby felt her knees start to tremble and her arms start to shake. A beautiful, perfect baby. A little early maybe, but with the best care in the world. This little girl would have a better than average chance at life. But what about her own precious bundle? What would Reuben's chances be? Her head started to swim.

'Do you still need me, Linc?'

He looked up from where he was making a few notes and shook his head. 'No, everything's fine here. I'll give you a call if I need a hand.' He took in her pale expression. 'Are you okay, Abby?'

She nodded wordlessly and pushed her way out of the room, her legs on autopilot as she strode down the corridor. Her hand reached into her pocket and she pulled out the hospital letter with Reuben's appointment on it. She needed air. She needed clean, fresh air that you could only get from being outside.

All of a sudden she couldn't be in there. But why now? Why, when it was probably the most important birth of the year? She hadn't felt this way when she'd seen Valerie Carter's new baby boy yesterday. But then again, she hadn't witnessed the birth. She hadn't seen the commitment and love of two devoted parents getting their first chance to hold their child—the child that would quickly become the centre of their whole universe.

And it made her want to cry. Because her little boy didn't have that. He didn't have two devoted parents and the best expert care in the world. He had one scared-out-of-her-wits mom.

'Abby…'

She heard the voice shout her name, but ignored it, throwing open the outside door and walking out into the streaming sunshine. She tried to take some deep breaths, to fill her lungs and calm her heartbeat.

Seconds later a pair of arms swept around her, then a hand brushed her blonde hair from her eyes. 'Are you okay, Abby? Did something happen to the baby?'

Luke's voice was filled with concern, his arms supporting most of her weight while her legs were buckling under her. He pulled her over to the nearby bench outside the front doors of the hospital.

She sat for a few seconds, her eyes fixed on the horizon, her trembling hands in her lap. The hospital appointment card was screwed into a ball in her hands. 'The baby's fine, Luke. It's a girl. And she's perfect.'

The words broke her. Broke her last few seconds of stern resolve and she dissolved into tears.

And Luke just knew. Knew exactly what was wrong. The irony of the perfect baby wasn't lost on him. Not while Abby feared for her son's life.

He gathered her into his arms and stroked her hair. 'One more day, Abby. Just get through today and we'll find out tomorrow.' He could feel the tension in her shoulders, the strain in her face.

'I can't do this,' she whispered. 'I can't lose my baby.'

'Stop thinking the worst. This might only be a minor setback. The bruises—they might just be that, bruises. It might not mean anything.'

The words made her angry, as if he wasn't taking this seriously. She sat up. 'You don't know that. *I* don't know that. Tell me something. Did you manage to get a good night's sleep last night? Because I didn't—I couldn't sleep a wink.'

Her frustration was coming to a head now. 'And don't say "we". Don't say that as if you're going to be here—you're not. I can't rely on you, Luke. I can't *let* myself rely on you. This isn't your life. It's mine.' She stood up now and started pacing around. 'You don't even like Reuben that much. Do you think I don't know how awkward you feel around him? How much of a struggle it is for you to spend time with him?'

The whole world seemed to be exploding around her right now. Luke's reappearance, Reuben's threat of illness. And it was all *her* fault. She'd allowed him to slip back into her life. Because the truth was, she'd never stopped loving him. That's why she'd never found room in her heart for anyone else. And from the second he'd walked through the doors of the ER everything had just fallen into place.

And right now it all just seemed so *wrong*.

Luke hadn't moved. He sat on the bench and watched her pacing. She was venting her frustration and he knew that. Hell—he'd been there and worn the T-shirt. But she was right. And it was embarrassing.

He bit his lip. A voice echoed in his head—Ryan. *Speak now or for ever hold your peace.* They'd always joked that they would like to have walked into a wedding at that point and said something—anything—to the shocked congregation. How could he explain this?

'Abby, it's not that I don't like Reuben. I do like him. I do.'

'Then what is it?' Her voice was clipped.

He swept his arms outwards. 'It's everything. It's all of this. He's just...so familiar to me. I feel as if I'm getting the chance to relive part of my life with Ryan all over again. And I know that's wrong. He's not Ryan—he's Reuben—and I'm trying really hard not to get the two mixed up.' He ran his fingers through his hair. His eyes met hers and he held his hand out towards her. 'And then there's you.'

She kept her arms firmly by her sides. 'What does that mean?'

He stepped closer, putting his hands on either side of her waist. 'This.' He bent his head and kissed her gently on the nose. 'I can't separate out how I feel about you from all this.'

She shook her head. 'I don't understand…'

'You're a package deal now, Abby, and I know that. I can't have one without the other.'

Her hands started to shake again. 'You're absolutely right, Luke, you can't. So what do you mean—you can't have one without the other?' She stepped back to distance herself from him.

'You would prefer it if Reuben wasn't here, wouldn't you?'

He hesitated, for just a fraction too long as he tried to find the right words.

The tears streamed down her cheeks. 'I'm trying to face up to the fact my little boy might be having a relapse of his illness—one that could steal him away from me—and you wish he wasn't here? What kind of a person are you?'

'Abby, no...' He reached out to touch her, but she jumped backwards.

'Don't touch me! Don't touch me again, ever! You're right, I am a package deal. It's not enough that you have feelings for me. I need you to love Reuben too. I need to know that if something happened to me tomorrow, you would be willing to step in and be there for him—not wish him away!'

'You're putting words into my mouth that I never said.'

'You didn't have to say them, I can see them in your eyes!'

He shook his head. 'You're wrong, Abby. That's not what you see. You're not the only one that's scared here.'

'Scared of what?'

'Scared of losing something that's infinitely precious to me. I've been there—and barely survived. I don't know if I can do that again. What happens if I love Reuben and I lose him too? What happens if I watch you fall apart before my eyes? Do you think there's anything about this that's easy?' He was suddenly conscious of the fact he was shouting. The more upset he'd become, the louder his voice.

He looked out towards the sea. 'This isn't about the fact I'm awkward around kids. I am, and I know I am. When I knew I couldn't have children I distanced myself from them. I didn't really want to know what I was missing out on. Because that just makes it tougher to take. I'm not entirely sure what a four-year-old wants in this world. I'm trying to relate to Reuben, really I am. But I can only base what I know on my own memories— memories of me and my brother.'

His mouth curled upwards. 'But Reuben's different. The likeness to Ryan aside, he's not your average kid and I've spent the last few days seeing that.'

He took her hands in his and pulled her back over towards the bench. 'I want to be here for you, Abby. I want to be your friend.'

She took a sharp intake of breath. A friend. What did that mean exactly? This was all too much. She didn't have the time or energy to waste on this right now. She needed to focus. She needed to prioritise.

She pulled her hands backwards into her lap, as

if she was trying to put some distance between them. 'You've confused things for me, Luke. I thought I had everything I wanted here. Then you appeared and...' Her words trailed off. She shook her head. 'I need to concentrate on Reuben right now. We've got an appointment tomorrow at San Fran Children's Hospital.' Her voice grew quiet. 'I've no idea what will happen, but right now...' she raised her eyes again to meet his '...I need to be a mom.'

His hand reached over and stroked her cheek. 'I wouldn't want you to be anything else, Abby. Being a mom is what I always wanted for you. You were made for this job.'

Her face changed and he couldn't read it. A multitude of expressions flitted across her face as she obviously processed her feelings. Her eyes fixed on the screwed-up ball of paper still in her hand. Luke felt as if he was on a cliff edge, dangling, waiting for the right or wrong words that could send him tumbling into oblivion. If only he could say what she really needed to hear. That he loved her and he needed her. And that he could be there to hold Reuben's hand no matter what the outcome. But he had to be sure. He had to be absolutely sure that this was something he could do. And the one person he could talk to about all this wasn't here.

Ryan. Ryan only existed in his head now. He didn't have him to laugh and joke with, to ask advice, to lend a sympathetic ear. And Abby was the person who would naturally fill that role for him now. She was the person who knew him best. So why couldn't he talk to her about this? Why couldn't he make her understand?

She looked so lost. And alone. Alone, with the weight of the world on her shoulders.

Noise surrounded them. A siren, approaching fast. He watched as a police car pulled up at the entrance, closely followed by a procession of sleek black cars. He jumped up and ran over to the police chief. 'Is something wrong?'

The police chief took a second to give his badge a cursory glance, before watching as an array of men in black exited the cars. James Turner strode through the main entrance, his hand outstretched towards the chief.

'Thanks for coming.'

Luke looked from one to the other. 'What on earth is going on?'

James Turner raised his eyebrow. 'Word's got out about the First Lady. We're just about to turn this into a no-fly zone. Our plans have changed. We need to resecure this area.'

'What does that mean?'

The police chief shook his head. 'Before, no one knew the First Lady was here. Now the media have hired every moveable object in the area and are trying to reach the hospital. The President's here, so the whole area above Pelican Cove needs to be declared a no-fly zone for security reasons. It's going to be chaos around here. And now we have a baby to protect too.'

Luke took a deep breath. This was the last thing they needed. He glanced over his shoulder towards Abby. She'd heard every word.

'I'll try and clear the ER.' She headed back inside. Their conversation was clearly over.

She strode away from him and Luke watched as the crumpled hospital appointment rolled across the ground at her feet, like a tumbleweed ball across a desert.

CHAPTER ELEVEN

ABBY bent down and zipped up Reuben's red raincoat. 'Ready, honey?'

He shook his blond head and glared at her with his pale blue eyes. 'Don't want to go,' he said stubbornly.

She knew exactly how he felt. She lifted her hand and traced her finger down his cheek. 'I don't want to go either, honey, but we have to. We have to find out if you need more special medicine.'

'I don't need any special medicine.' He raised his arms to show her his muscles, hidden under layers of clothes. 'Look, Mommy, I'm strong, I don't need any.'

Abby smiled at his bravado. Reuben wasn't a child who screamed and shouted and had temper tantrums. He liked to argue his case with her. See if he could win her round. But he could never win this argument.

This morning she could see just how pale he

was. He had hardly eaten any dinner last night—
even though she'd made his favourite—and even
though she'd tried to tempt him with an early
breakfast this morning, it had been a washout.
She could tell right now that he was still tired and
he would probably fall asleep in the car on the way
to San Francisco.

She put her hands around him and pulled him
up into her arms. 'I know you're strong, Reuben. *I*
think you're the strongest boy in the world. And do
you know what? When we finish up at the hospital
today, I'm going to take you to the big toy shop
and you can pick another wrestler for your ring.
How's that?'

'How many?' The immediate distraction worked.
Four-year-olds knew exactly where their priorities
lay.

Abby wrinkled her nose as she lifted her bag
and pulled the front door open. 'Maybe one, no…
maybe two, or…if you're extra good,' she whispered in his ear, 'maybe three!'

'Whoopee!' Reuben flung his hands in the air
and laughed. 'Three new wrestlers!'

She caught a glimpse of a shape. A dark figure

on her front steps that leapt to his feet as they came through the door. She stopped short. Luke.

'What are you doing here?'

He hadn't stayed there last night and she'd no idea where he'd been. How long had he been sitting there?

'Waiting for you.'

'Hi, Luke. Mommy's going to buy me some new wrestlers today. Wanna come?'

Abby glanced at her watch. She had plenty of time to spare, but she didn't want to spend it on this. 'I can't deal with you today, Luke.' She pushed past him towards her car, pressing the button to open the doors.

His hand closed over hers, releasing the key from her grasp. 'I'm not here to fight with you, but I am coming with you. Let me drive.'

'In that?' She pointed towards her Mini, her eyes running up and down his tall frame. 'You won't even fit.'

He eyed the car carefully and gave a slow nod. 'I'll get in there if I have to bend myself double.' He pulled open the nearest door. 'Why don't you sit in the back with Reuben? Let me take the stress of the drive. San Francisco can be pretty hairy at this time of day.'

She bit her lip. She hated driving to San Francisco. She hated driving full stop. That was part of the reason she loved Pelican Cove so much, she hardly had to use her car at all.

He lowered his voice. 'I'm not going to let you go alone, Abby. I'm not going to let you go through this yourself today. You don't have to. I want to be here. Let me help you.' His eyes were fixed on hers with an air of determination she'd never seen before. She could spend the next hour arguing with him and still wouldn't win, and somehow she didn't want to. She really didn't want to spend the day alone in the hospital, waiting to hear the news that she dreaded.

'C'mon, Mommy. Let's go get the wrestlers.' Reuben shifted in her arms, causing her to snap to attention.

'Will we let Luke come with us?' she asked him.

'Is he going to buy me a wrestler too?'

She laughed. Life was so simple when you were four years old. 'Okay, then, you can come.' She held Luke's gaze for a second. 'But don't make this any harder for me.'

'I won't, I promise.' He nodded solemnly before she finally turned and loaded Reuben into the car seat, strapping him in place before joining him in the back seat. Luke folded himself into her tiny car, pushing the seat back against her legs, before starting the engine and heading down the cliff-side road towards the city.

Within ten minutes Reuben was sleeping—just like she'd predicted. Another sign. That was three this morning. He was pale, tired and he'd lost his appetite. None of this was good.

Things weren't meant to work out like this. She'd been so hopeful. After all, the majority of kids with ALL now had good outcomes. Was she going to have one of the unfortunate few?

He was in his third phase of treatment. He'd had the awful induction therapy to kill all the affected cells, then he'd had his consolidation therapy to kill any remaining cells that could grow again and cause a relapse. Now he was in the maintenance phase. Maintenance that for Reuben obviously hadn't worked. She was going to have to go through all this again. Weeks of sickness, weeks of avoiding infection, weeks of a little boy who was so tired he could barely keep his eyes open.

Weeks of finding him something, *anything,* that he might be able to stomach and keep down. It wouldn't be the first time she'd bundled him up in the car and left the house in the dead of night in search of some type of popsicle or chocolate bar that he'd decided he could eat.

She turned and looked out of the window as the perfect ocean views of Pelican Cove drifted past. The crashing waves, rugged coastline and lush green hills. She'd wanted the perfect life here. She'd wanted to bring her child up here—but was this the place her child could die?

The thought sent an involuntary shudder down her spine and she could feel the rise of bile in the back of her throat. Where did these thoughts come from? How did they get inside her mind? Inside her dreams? Last night had been a repeat of the little white coffin, being lowered into the ground. But last night's dream had changed. This time Luke had been standing next to her, his arms wrapped around her shoulders.

Was it a prediction? Was she seeing the future? Because this wasn't the future she wanted. She couldn't even contemplate a future like that.

Another thought played across her mind. If something happened to Reuben, would she even want to be here any more? Their lives were so entrenched, so intermingled, she couldn't imagine living without him. Someone had once told her that parents shouldn't outlive their children. She hadn't understood the significance of the words at the time. But now she did. She wouldn't want to be here without him. She *couldn't* be here without him. How could she stay in her aunt's house without every thought being of him? It was a happy home and should be filled with a happy family.

If she didn't have her son, what was there to live for? Having Luke here wasn't enough, no matter how much she loved him. She needed them both. She needed a whole family, a complete family, because, truth be told, right now she was terrified and she didn't think she could go through all this again on her own.

Her breath caught in her throat. What was happening to her? Was she losing her mind? She'd never had thoughts like this in her life. She had to focus. She had to concentrate. She had to get through today.

Luke pulled into the car park and breathed an audible sigh of relief. Ninety minutes of almost complete silence. Not a word, just the easy-listening tunes on the radio as background noise.

He opened the door and stepped out, hearing the loud crick in his neck as he arched his back and stretched his cramped legs. He opened the back door, unclipped Reuben and lifted him out. The little boy didn't even wake up, just snuggled into the nape of his neck. And this time Luke didn't pull away. This felt natural.

Abby stepped out the other side, her eyes fixed on the large metropolitan building in front of them.

'Okay?' he asked. She nodded and walked back around the car, her hand reaching up and stroking Reuben's sleeping head.

There was something strange about being in a hospital where nobody knew who you were—you were just another face in the crowd. None of the usual nods of recognition or waves or greetings that usually happened. No one searching for you to consult on a patient or provide medical expertise.

It was strangely disconcerting. Luke rarely told people outside the workplace that he was a doctor—a safeguard mechanism against them listing all their medical complaints for him. But this time he wanted people to know. He wanted them to know he was a doctor, he understood the language, the jargon and to appreciate the knowledge and skills he must have.

He smiled to himself. Was this what happened? Was this the type of feelings that swamped you when you wanted to be an advocate for your child?

Abby was obviously familiar with the place. She wove through the endless white corridors until they reached a set of lifts. Luke moved inside and waited while she pressed the button. The lift moved upwards silently. The doors swooshed open.

And then it hit him. Like an assault. That *smell*. The smell that could only be associated with this type of ward. Paediatric oncology.

It assaulted his senses in a way he'd never expected, bringing with it an onslaught of unexpected memories. Tests, procedures, medications, dressings. And waiting. Endless and endless waiting.

He must have flinched. 'Luke?' Abby's face was wary. She pressed the button to stop the lift doors sliding shut again. 'Are you getting out?' she said pointedly.

He nodded and quickly stepped out of the lift and into the ward. They walked down the corridor, passing open doors showing kids of all ages, sleeping, playing, crying, eating, all at various stages of disease and recovery. For Luke, he'd just stepped back in time. His fingers tightened around Reuben's sleeping form. He didn't want to let him go.

The brightly coloured murals on the walls passed by in a flash. A woman in a bright pink tunic walked over and kissed Abby on the cheek. 'Hi, Abby, how's he doing?' She walked around to Luke's shoulder and smiled at the sleeping boy. She held out her arms. 'How about I take him while you go in and speak to Jonas?'

Abby nodded at Luke and he reluctantly handed over the sleeping bundle. A sandy-haired man opened the door to the office in front of them. 'Hi, Abby, I thought I heard Toni's voice. Come on in.'

His eyes fell on Luke as he held the office door open for them both.

Abby sat down in one of the nearby chairs. 'Jonas, this is Dr Luke Storm, he's a…family friend.'

Jonas's eyes narrowed slightly at her hesitation before he extended his hand towards Luke's and shook it firmly.

'Pleased to meet you, Luke. Jonas Bridges. I'm glad that Abby has someone here to support her.'

He sat down at his desk and pushed some forms across the desk towards Abby. Reuben's blood test results. Did that seem cold? Luke wasn't sure. But Abby had obviously been seeing this doctor regarding Reuben's care for a long time. Maybe it was just the professional mutual respect of them both being doctors that led him to be so straightforward?

Luke leaned across the desk and peered at the result. It was just as they feared. Not good.

'What kind of doctor are you, Luke? Is this your field?' Jonas was obviously trying to feel his way, to see how much explaining he would need to do.

Luke shook his head. 'No, this isn't my field. I'm a cardiologist. But…' he glanced back at Abby, whose eyes were still fixed on the blood results '…I've probably got a better understanding of these than most people. My brother had ALL fifteen years ago.'

Jonas nodded slowly, obviously digesting the information. His steady gaze held Luke's. 'And now?'

Luke gave an imperceptible shake of his head.

'I'm sorry to hear that.' His hands reached across the desk and clasped Abby's. 'You know what I'm going to tell you next. We need to do another bone-marrow aspiration today. I know that you've probably prepared Reuben for that, but I want to take some time to speak to him myself before we do the procedure. Is that okay with you?'

She gave a weak smile. 'I thought you might.'

'I'll be honest with you, Abby, and I think you know what we will find. Depending on what the bone-marrow aspiration shows, it's likely we're going to have to look at another round of treatment for Reuben.'

'What kind?' Her voice was quiet, almost a whisper.

Jonas's voice was steady and calm. 'We'll discuss the options. We might go for another round of chemotherapy, we might look at chemotherapy with stem-cell transplant, I might also recommend that Reuben takes part in one of our specialised clinical trials.'

Luke was nodding slowly. Dr Bridges was laying out the options so that nothing would be a surprise for her. Just like any reliable physician should. Just as he would. He could see that from a professional perspective. But this didn't feel like his normal professional consultations. All of Luke's emotions were heightened. This was Reuben they were talking about. But they might as well have been talking about Ryan—because this felt personal.

Jonas pushed a consent form in front of Abby with Reuben's name and the procedure listed on it. 'I know you're a doctor, Abby, but today you're a parent—like any other. Do you want me to talk you through this again?'

She shook her head silently and scribbled her name on the consent form.

'I take it you haven't given him breakfast this morning Abby?'

She shook her head again. The words just wouldn't come to her lips right now. She'd already fasted him, knowing the strong likelihood of the procedure taking place. 'I woke him extra-early and planned to give him something light, but he wasn't hungry. He couldn't eat.'

Jonas took one last look over his notes. 'It will only be a really light anaesthetic, Abby—just like last time. And you'll be able to take him home in a few hours as long as his pain is under control. Do you want to come in with him again?'

Abby nodded then stood up, pushing her chair backwards. 'Do you want to speak to Reuben first, then?'

Jonas nodded. 'Give me a few minutes then come into the room. Toni, the nurse, has everything set up for us.'

Abby folded her arms across her chest and moved sideways to let Jonas past. She didn't speak. She didn't say anything. She didn't even turn to face him.

Luke stood up and wrapped his arm around her shoulders. Her head naturally leaned against him. 'He hates this part,' she whispered.

So did Luke. He'd been with Ryan four times when he'd had a bone-marrow aspiration done. It wasn't a pleasant experience for a teenager, let alone for a child. 'He's a good kid, Abby, he'll get through this.'

'But will I?' The question hung in the air between them.

Had she meant to say that out loud? Was that just another random thought that was circulating around her brain? Luke wasn't quite sure how to respond.

He felt his shoulders tense, a ripple of fear dancing along the edge of his stomach. Memories of his own mother's actions. What had happened to steadfast Abby?

This was hard. This was difficult. But she was Reuben's mom. Of course she would get through this—no matter how hard it was.

The door creaked and Toni appeared at their side. 'Do you want to come through? Jonas has spoken to Reuben and he's a little upset about the test.'

Abby nodded swiftly and turned, striding out the door. Just as she should. So what had happened a few seconds ago?

Abby couldn't think straight. She was a doctor. She was used to these things. She'd had to have numerous conversations like this with parents over the years. She hadn't even needed to see the blood results—because she'd known what they would show.

But somehow it made it all worse. They were real. Her son's leukaemia was back. The maintenance phase was over—it hadn't worked. And in the cold, hard light of day, having the figures in front of her in black and white just...sucked.

A word she hadn't used since she was a teenager. But right now it was the only way to describe how she felt.

She didn't want to think of any of the other descriptive words. Terrified. Shocked. Traumatised.

She took a deep breath and walked into the treatment room.

'Mommy!'

Reuben was sitting on the edge of the examination couch, his arms extended towards her. She walked over and enveloped him in a bear hug. His eyes were watery. 'I need the big needle again, Mommy,' he whispered in her ear.

She knelt down before him. 'I know, honey. But Mommy will stay with you and Dr Jonas will have it all over in a flash. Just think about those lovely wrestlers you want to pick later today.'

Toni came in with a brightly coloured robe in her hands. 'I brought you your favourite one, Reuben—with the monkeys on it.' She turned to face Abby. 'Do you want to get him changed or shall I?'

Abby lifted the robe from her hands. 'I'll do it. Do you know if they will be long?'

Toni shook her head. 'Less than ten minutes. Jonas is away to scrub and the anaesthetist will be through in a couple of minutes. I've brought some scrubs for you and your…friend,' her eyes ran up and down the length of Luke. 'Do you both want to be here?'

She turned and gave Luke a smile. 'We try to make this as informal as possible. Parents are encouraged to stay with their children throughout, so they can better understand the procedure. And the anaesthetic is very light, just knocks them out for fifteen minutes or so.'

Luke smiled and took the scrubs from her hands. Toni hadn't been in the consulting room. She'd no idea he knew this stuff like the back of his hand. And she still hadn't asked about his relationship to Reuben. Was she making an assumption because of their looks?

'We're both staying,' he said decidedly.

Toni gave a nod and left them both to change. Abby ducked into the nearby washroom and came out with her hair tied back from her face and the pale blue scrubs on.

'Go and get ready,' she said quietly as she bent over Reuben and started dispensing with his jeans.

Luke came out in time to meet the anaesthetist and listen to her laugh and joke with Reuben as she explained about the little mask she'd use to make him sleepy. Luke wondered how it must feel to have to do this every day. To have to look after sick children and their parents.

Jonas Bridges appeared back in the room, scrubbed and ready to start. He gave a little nod to the anaesthetist, who lifted the mask above Reuben's face. Seconds later, his hand still ensconced in Abby's, Reuben was fast asleep.

The staff moved seamlessly and like clockwork. Reuben was turned on his side, positioned so the posterior iliac spine of the pelvic bone was revealed. A few sweeps with antiseptic and they were ready.

Abby swallowed the enormous lump that had appeared in her throat. Reuben was sleeping and she watched as Jonas injected some lidocaine into the area around the site to help with Reuben's pain control later.

His gloved hands removed the needle from its

protective covering and prodded Reuben's skin to determine where to insert it.

She felt something wash over her. The same feeling that had swept over her in that room in Pelican Cove when the First Lady had had her baby. Like a warm summer heat enveloping her skin. But it wasn't comforting. It was restricting. It was clawing at her throat and her lungs. She gave a little cough as she tried to pull in some air.

But it wasn't working. The nausea from earlier returned with a vengeance. Gripping at her stomach muscles, making her retch. She lifted her hand to her mouth. Luke's eyes turned to her, narrowing instantly.

The room was closing in on her. How could anyone breathe in here? There was no air. It was suffocating. Tingling sensations started in the palms of her hands and crept up her arms towards her chest. Her heart was racing, liked a trapped butterfly beating frantically inside her chest.

Her eyes darted around the room. Why was everyone else okay? Didn't they feel it too? Were the anaesthetic gases leaking?

The voices inside her head started playing automatically. *Calm down. Calm down.*

But she couldn't. She was going to die in here. Her skin was covered in sweat, she could feel rivulets running down her spine and catching in the waistband of her scrubs.

Her eyes fixed on Reuben lying on the examination couch. His short white-blond hair and pale skin. Such an angel. Reuben looked like an angel.

Angel. Death.

She had to get out of here. She couldn't be in here. Whatever it was, it was going to kill her. She dropped Reuben's hand from hers and pulled back from the side of the couch. Try as she might, she couldn't get a breath. She couldn't fill her lungs with air. Her head swam. She was dizzy. She was going to be sick.

Luke placed his strong arm on hers. His voice full of concern. 'Abby?'

It didn't sound right. His voice sounded distorted, as if it belonged to someone else. She tried to take a step backwards and staggered, reaching out behind her to grab hold of the wall.

'I have to go,' she muttered as she stumbled towards the door.

'Wait a minute, Abby. What's wrong?' Luke's arms gripped her shoulders, his face directly in front of hers. But it was swimming. It wasn't staying in one place. And he was right in front of her, stealing the air that she so desperately needed to breathe. She pushed him with all her might, sending him backwards towards Reuben.

She grasped at her throat as she pulled at the doorhandle. What was happening to her?

The last thing she saw was Luke's eyes, looking at her with pure venom as she wrenched open the door and headed for the clean, fresh air.

CHAPTER TWELVE

LUKE couldn't believe what he'd just witnessed. Abby—the person who loved her child more than anything—had just run out on him.

She was just his mother all over again. Running out on her child when he needed her most. What kind of parent did that?

His reaction was instantaneous. He moved over towards the examination couch and put his hand in Reuben's. He was still anesthetised, still sleeping. He would have no idea what had just happened. The little boy's skin was cool, so he brought his other hand over and gently rubbed some heat into him.

He was aware of the guarded looks around him. The unspoken messages passing between the various members of staff.

Toni, the nurse, touched his shoulder. 'Do you want to go after her?'

'No.' His voice was brusque. He wasn't going anywhere. His job was here, with Reuben.

Jonas looked up from where he was extracting the bone-marrow aspirate. 'I'll be finished in a few minutes. Then we can wake Reuben up again.'

Luke captured the look in his eyes. The knowledge, the expertise.

Jonas was still looking at him, his voice quiet. 'It happens quite a lot, you know.'

'People run out on their kids?'

Jonas arched an eyebrow at him, before he looked downwards again, slowly removed the needle from Reuben's hip and pressed down firmly on the site.

'No. Parents panic. This might seem like a relatively simple procedure. But the results mean a whole lot more. Sometimes the magnitude of the situation doesn't hit a parent until they're in here. And they realise that the result of this test could be the difference between life and death for their child. You said you've been through this before. You should understand.'

Lord, the man was brutal. He didn't mince his words. Should he really be working in a place like this?

Luke bit his lip. He lifted his hand and stroked Reuben's fine blond hair and ran a finger gently down his cheek. This little boy needed someone. This little boy needed *him*.

Jonas covered the area with a dressing, snapped off his gloves and walked around the bed towards Luke. He pressed a firm hand on his shoulder. 'Once she's calmed down, Abby will be distraught about what just happened. If you know her at all, you know that about her.'

Something twisted inside him. He was a doctor. He knew the signs. He should have recognised them quicker. Abby had had a panic attack. She hadn't run out on her child. She would *never* run out on her child. So why was he so furious?

Luke ran his fingers through his hair. 'I can't leave Reuben. I need to be here for Reuben.'

The anaesthetist gave him a nod. 'We're done here. I'm just waking him up. Why don't you wait until he comes to, then go and find his mom?'

He nodded as she removed the anaesthetic mask. 'He's had some local anaesthetic in the site and he's been given some pain relief so hopefully he'll be quite comfortable when he wakes up. You can let us know if he needs anything else.'

Luke nodded slowly. The air in the room was quiet, his large hand was still holding Reuben's small one —and he'd no intention of letting go.

* * *

Abby felt the cool breeze rustle through her hair. She could hear the sounds of bubbling water. Her heart had stopped clamouring. Her head had stopped spinning. She could finally breathe again. Where was she?

She slowly lifted her head from between her knees. She was outside the hospital entrance, in the gardens at the front, sitting on one of the benches next to the ornamental fountain. How had she got here?

She put her hands on her waist, arched her back and took a deep breath. It was a beautiful warm sunny day but she was cold. Her hand touched the thin blue scrubs she was wearing. They were damp. No wonder she was cold.

Her mind shifted and things came back into focus. Oh, no. Reuben. How was Reuben?

She jumped from the seat, but her legs were unprepared and they buckled underneath her. She had to get back up there. She had to see how her son was. Her eyes turned towards the hospital building. The light was reflecting off the tinted glass windows, causing it to blind her. A tall figure was striding purposefully across the grass towards her. She raised her hand to shield her eyes from the sun.

Luke. Her insides curled. What must he think of her? She cringed as she remembered the look on his face when he'd told her about his mother and the day she'd run out on Ryan when he'd been having his bone-marrow aspiration done. The disgust. The absolute disgust and contempt he'd felt. And now he'd feel that way about her.

She pushed back against the hard wooden bench. Would he yell? Would he scream at her? He couldn't possibly make her feel any worse than she did now.

The figure came into focus. Like her, still dressed in the hospital blue scrubs. His tall frame blocked out the sunlight as he came towards her. She could stop squinting now and focus on his face.

It was blank. Unreadable. Had something happened to Reuben?

'Luke…'

His hand reached out and touched her shoulder. 'Reuben's fine, Abby.' He'd sensed her immediate fears and quelled them. He removed his hand and sat down next to her, the bench shifting underneath her at the weight, his hands clasped in front of him.

'I don't know what to say. I don't know what happened in there. I couldn't breathe. It was claustrophobic. I thought I was going to be sick—or pass out.' The words shot out, one after another.

His hand reached over and touched her leg. It was warm, providing heat through her sweat-drenched scrubs. 'You had a panic attack, Abby.'

She shook her head. 'That's ridiculous. I'm a doctor. Why on earth would I have a panic attack?' But even as she said the words of denial, the pieces of the jigsaw puzzle started to fall into place.

'Because you're not a doctor here, Abby.' He waved his arm towards the building. 'This isn't Pelican Cove. Here you're a mom, with the possibility of a sick child. *That's* why you had a panic attack.' His lips turned upwards in a rueful smile. 'It doesn't have to make sense, you know.'

She groaned. 'I think I'm going to be sick.' She ducked her head down between her knees, waiting for the wave of nausea to pass again. Luke's hand was on her back, stroking her neck.

He was touching her. He wasn't shouting. He

wasn't yelling. She felt the tears brim in her eyes. What did that mean?

Her head flipped back up and she took a deep breath. She studied his face carefully. 'You must hate me.'

He shifted uncomfortably. 'What makes you say that?'

'The way you looked at me when I left the room. I saw you. I could see in your eyes how you felt about me.'

Luke leaned forward and put his head in his hands.

She kept talking. 'I'm sorry, Luke. I know you told me about your mom leaving Ryan. I never, ever thought I would do the same thing.'

'What do you want me to say to you, Abby?'

'That you don't hate me—that you forgive me.'

Silence. Luke was studying the ground at his feet. 'I don't know if I can say that.' His words were quiet, whispered. 'You reminded me of every reason why I hate my mother today.'

Abby's voice caught in her throat. She couldn't hide the desperation in her voice, she was clutching at straws and she knew it. 'Do you think it's possible she had a panic attack too?'

Luke threw up his hands in exasperation. 'The woman would have to feel some kind of emotion to have a panic attack, Abby.'

'How can you say that? How can you *know* that? Did you ever speak to her about it?' She was tired, tired of Luke for judging her and judging his mother.

He jumped up from the bench. 'Talk to her about it? You must be joking. If I wanted to talk to my mother about Ryan dying I'd have had to schedule an appointment in her diary!'

Abby could feel the anger rise in her veins. She jumped up too. 'And you think I'm like her? I'm like your mother? Do you know what I saw in that room, Luke? Do you know what's been haunting my dreams for the past few nights? Coffins. Little white coffins. Little white coffins being lowered into the ground. And it kills me. I wake up and for a second I don't know if it's real or not. And it takes me a few seconds to separate fact from fiction. And every time it happens I wonder if it's a premonition. And here…' she thrust a finger toward her chest '…right here, I know that if Reuben dies, I want to die with him.'

Luke opened his mouth and then stopped. The

pieces of the jigsaw puzzle in his mind finally slotted into place. This was it. This was what it felt like to have two people more precious to you than anything else in this world. This is what it felt like to have two people you would offer to sacrifice your own life for. To take their place—no matter what.

Abby stood before him, her pale skin almost translucent, her eyes strained, her hair in disarray and a multitude of tears spilling down her cheeks. She had never looked more beautiful and it twisted something deep inside his gut.

He took her arm and led her back to the bench, giving them both a few moments to collect their thoughts. He took a deep breath. 'You're not my mom, Abby.'

'But do you hate me? Will Reuben hate me?' Her bottom lip was trembling.

'Reuben doesn't even know, Abby. He's upstairs with Toni right now. I told him you'd stayed with him and went to the hospital store for a popsicle. He'll be expecting you any minute.'

She heaved a sigh of relief. The weight that had been pressing down on her chest beginning to subside. 'Thank you. Thank you, Luke.'

He saw her turn towards him, her face determined, her eyes steady. 'Why are you here? You gave up on me. You gave up on me and my ideas about a family for us. You wouldn't even try. I wasn't important enough for you to give us a shot.'

He shook his head, 'No Abby...'

But she stopped him. 'Why now, Luke? Why, when I'm probably at the most difficult stage in my life? Why have you decided you want to be part of my life now?'

She went to open her mouth again but he raised a hand to stop her. 'Let me speak. I've made a huge mistake. A mistake that started five years ago. I wanted you to be free to have a family of your own, the family you'd always dreamed about and the family that you deserved. I've made such a mess of this. These last few days, spending time with you and Reuben has been the best time of my life. I feel as if I've finally seen what a family could be, what a family *should* be. And I know, more than anything, that's what I want. I love you, Abby. I want you as my family, you and Reuben.'

He heard her sharp intake of breath. 'How can you say that after what just happened? How could you even contemplate loving me?'

'Because I never stopped. I love you, Abby. I love you and Reuben. I want to be part of your lives.'

'I love you too, Luke.' She shook her head. 'But this is just too hard.

'It isn't too hard.' His voice was determined. 'We won't let it be. You don't have to do this alone. Let me be there for you, for you and for Reuben.'

She shook her head. 'No, Luke. I can't expect that from you and why would you want to?' Her voice rose in confusion. 'You can walk away and not look back. You don't owe us anything.' His hand rested on her shoulder and her head automatically leaned towards it, finding comfort in its warmth. She placed her own hand over his. 'You've already been through this, Luke. You had a brother that you loved and lost. I couldn't ask you to do that again.'

He shook his head. 'This is different. I was a child myself back then, with two parents who couldn't deal with the situation. I'm an adult now, I'm free to make my own choices. And this is the choice that I choose to make. I only wish I'd been smart enough to be with you from the start of this. I don't want to walk away. I might not

284 THE BOY WHO MADE THEM LOVE AGAIN

be Reuben's father but I know what's here...' he
pointed towards his chest '...in my heart. For you
and for him.'

'But how can you?' Her voice wavered. 'How
can you choose to do this again?'

'Because the love always outweighs the pain.'
His voice was quiet and determined. 'No matter
what I went through with my brother, it was worth
it. *He* was worth it. I have millions of fabulous
memories of our time together. And if you told me
right now that I could have my life again, with or
without him in it, I would choose him every time.'

He put his finger under her chin and lifted her
head towards him. 'We don't know what will
happen with Reuben. But how much joy has he
brought you, Abby? Isn't he worth it?'

A single tear slid down her cheek. 'Of course he
is.'

'Then all I'm telling you is that you don't have
to do this alone. Because I think that you're worth
it, Abby. I think that Reuben's worth it too.' He
slid a finger through her blonde hair. 'You know
what they say—for better, for worse, for richer,
for poorer, in sickness and in health.' His voice

was trembling now; she knew what he was trying to say.

Her eyes were heavy with tears and she swallowed the lump in her throat that was the size of baseball. 'Can we do this in baby steps?'

'We can do this anyway you like.'

EPILOGUE

'I THINK I need an eternity ring.' Abby twisted the single diamond on her finger with the plain gold band underneath.

'What makes you think that?' Luke turned to face her, hoisting his hand under his head.

Abby stretched out on the blanket, lying on the grass in front of their house. She smiled as she watched Reuben play with his new brother. Austin, or the 'tiny terror' as they'd nicknamed him, was more than a match for his older brother. At the age of two, his ambition in life appeared to be to wreak havoc wherever he went. He'd only been with them for three weeks and so far he'd wrecked the sofa, gouged a hole in the dining-room table and trailed a black felt tip-pen along the pale cream wall in the hall.

Reuben was doing well. He'd had another course of treatment and been in remission for over a year. His energy had returned in leaps and bounds and he'd been over the moon at the prospect of a little brother.

She lifted her hand and let the sun's rays catch the diamond on her finger, glistening against the dark green grass. 'Some women get an eternity ring after they've been married a number of years. Some women get an eternity ring after the birth of their first child.' She waved her hand across the grass. 'Well, that's been over a year now, and I've got two kids, so cough up, mister.'

Luke reached his hand up and pulled the parasol a little lower, hiding them from the boys. 'Is this negotiable?' A wicked smile danced across his face. 'I might have bought you an alternative present.'

She sat upright. 'What do you mean?'

He took her hand in his and pulled her upwards, leading her towards the front door. She watched as he opened the cupboard directly inside the front door and heaved out a huge flat brown box, sliding it carefully across the floor.

Abby was amazed. When had this arrived? And how had she missed it? 'What is this?' she asked curiously.

'Open it and see.' He pulled a pair of scissors

from the drawer of the dresser that sat in the corridor.

She bent down and snipped at the heavy-duty string that was wrapped around it, peeling back the cardboard layers.

'Wow.'

A perfect round stained-glass window. To match the one at the other end of the upstairs corridor. But this one didn't have yellow daffodils and bluebells. This was the one she'd always imagined. This had a dazzling display of multicoloured freesias—colours that would send rainbow streams of light down her corridor.

'Oh, Luke, it's just perfect. More perfect than any ring could be.' Abby trailed a finger across his bare chest. The fire hadn't stilled between them, it just seemed to burn brighter and brighter.

'Good. Because I've been trying to keep that a secret for over a month. Now, what do I get in return?' he whispered in her ear.

Abby wriggled closer, loving the feel of his body against hers. 'Why, Dr Storm, you get me and two very noisy little boys—your very own fan club.' And she planted her lips on his, sealing their love with a kiss.

* * * * *